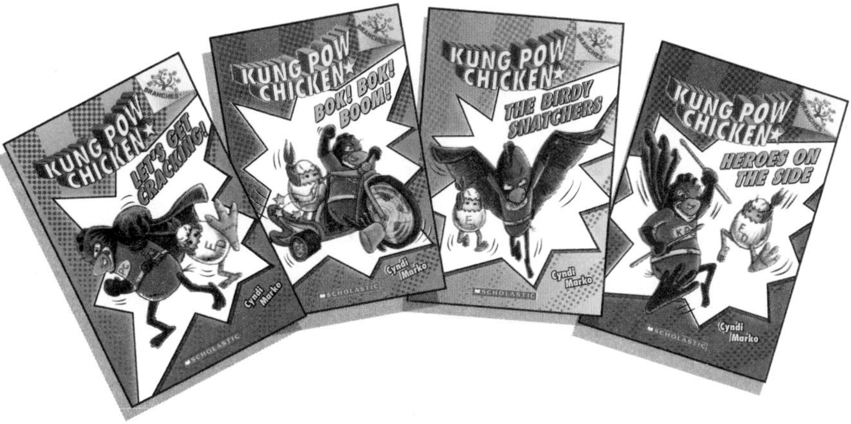
KUNG POW CHICKEN
LET'S GET CRACKING!
Cyndi Marko
SCHOLASTIC
KUNG POW CHICKEN
BOK! BOK! BOOM!
Cyndi Marko
SCHOLASTIC
KUNG POW CHICKEN
THE BIRDY SNATCHERS
Cyndi Marko
SCHOLASTIC
KUNG POW CHICKEN
HEROES ON THE SIDE
Cyndi Marko
SCHOLASTIC

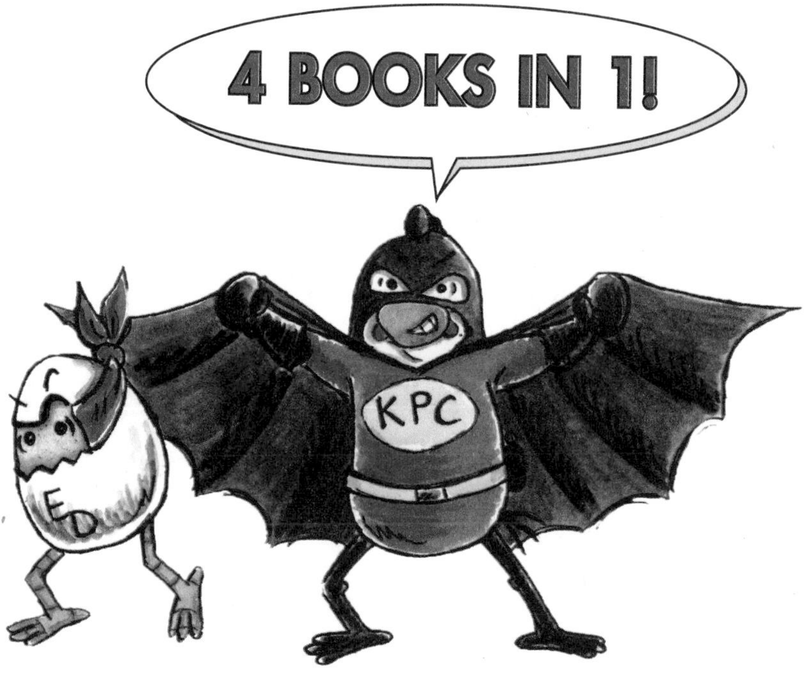
4 BOOKS IN 1!
KPC
ED

KUNG POW CHICKEN ★
COLLECTION

Cyndi Marko

BRANCHES
SCHOLASTIC INC.

ISBN 978-1-338-59921-3

10 9 8 7 6 5 4 3 2 1   20 21 22 23 24

Printed in the U.S.A.   40
First printing, April 2020
Edited by Katie Carella
Book Design by Marissa Asuncion

KUNG POW CHICKEN COLLECTION

TABLE OF CONTENTS

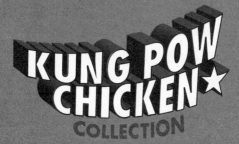

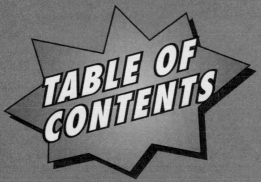

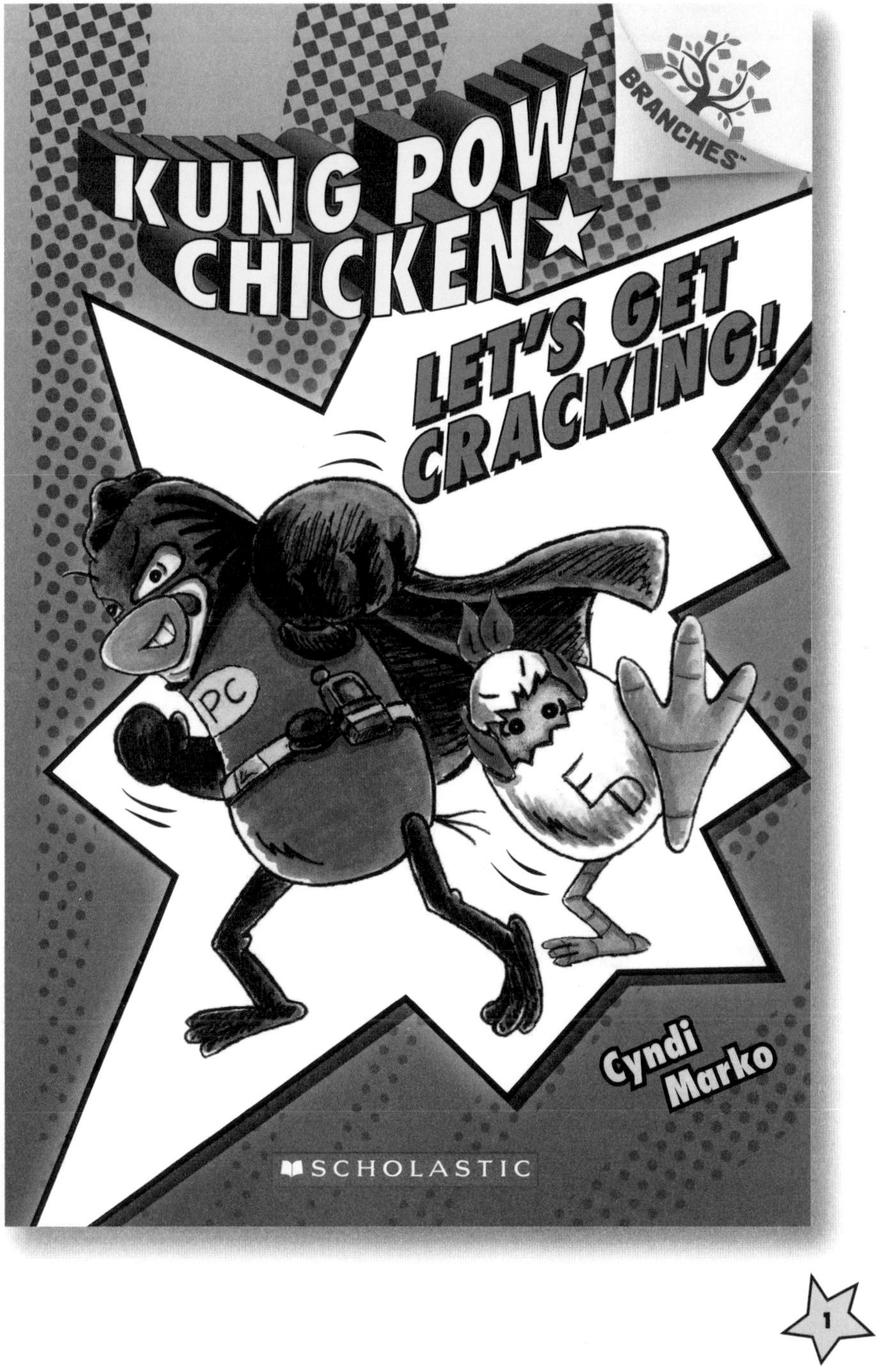
BRANCHES™
KUNG POW CHICKEN★
LET'S GET CRACKING!
PC
Cyndi Marko
SCHOLASTIC

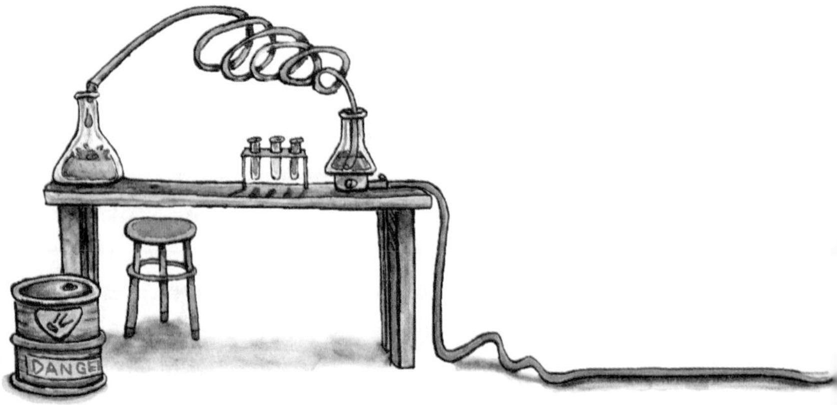
DANGE

TABLE OF CONTENTS

superhero poster

supersonic rocket

bunny slippers

drum

glasses comb beak wattle

wattle tail feathers school tie wing

drumsticks

chicken feet

Gordon Blue seemed like an ordinary chicken.

Gordon was in second grade at an ordinary school.

He lived in an ordinary house in the ordinary city of Fowladelphia. But he had a <u>super</u> secret.

Only Uncle Quack and Gordon's younger brother, Benedict, knew Gordon's secret.

Uncle Quack was a scientist. He worked in a lab.

One day when Gordon and Benny were younger, they had visited Uncle Quack at work.

Gordon and Benny started playing Follow the Leader. Gordon was in the lead and Benny followed every move Gordon made. Then . . .

. . . Gordon tripped and fell into a huge vat of bubbling toxic sludge! Benny followed Gordon's lead.

Uncle Quack quickly rescued his nephews.

But later Gordon started to feel strange. And as time passed he felt even stranger.

He tingled when danger was near.

He flapped his wings like the wind.

And he crowed louder than other chickens.
His bok was worse than his bite.

Gordon was no longer just an ordinary
chicken. The toxic sludge had given him
superpowers.

Hey, I got powers, too!
My shell is harder than
cafeteria cookies!

So Gordon made a super suit.

Hey, where's mine?

And Gordon came up with a super name:

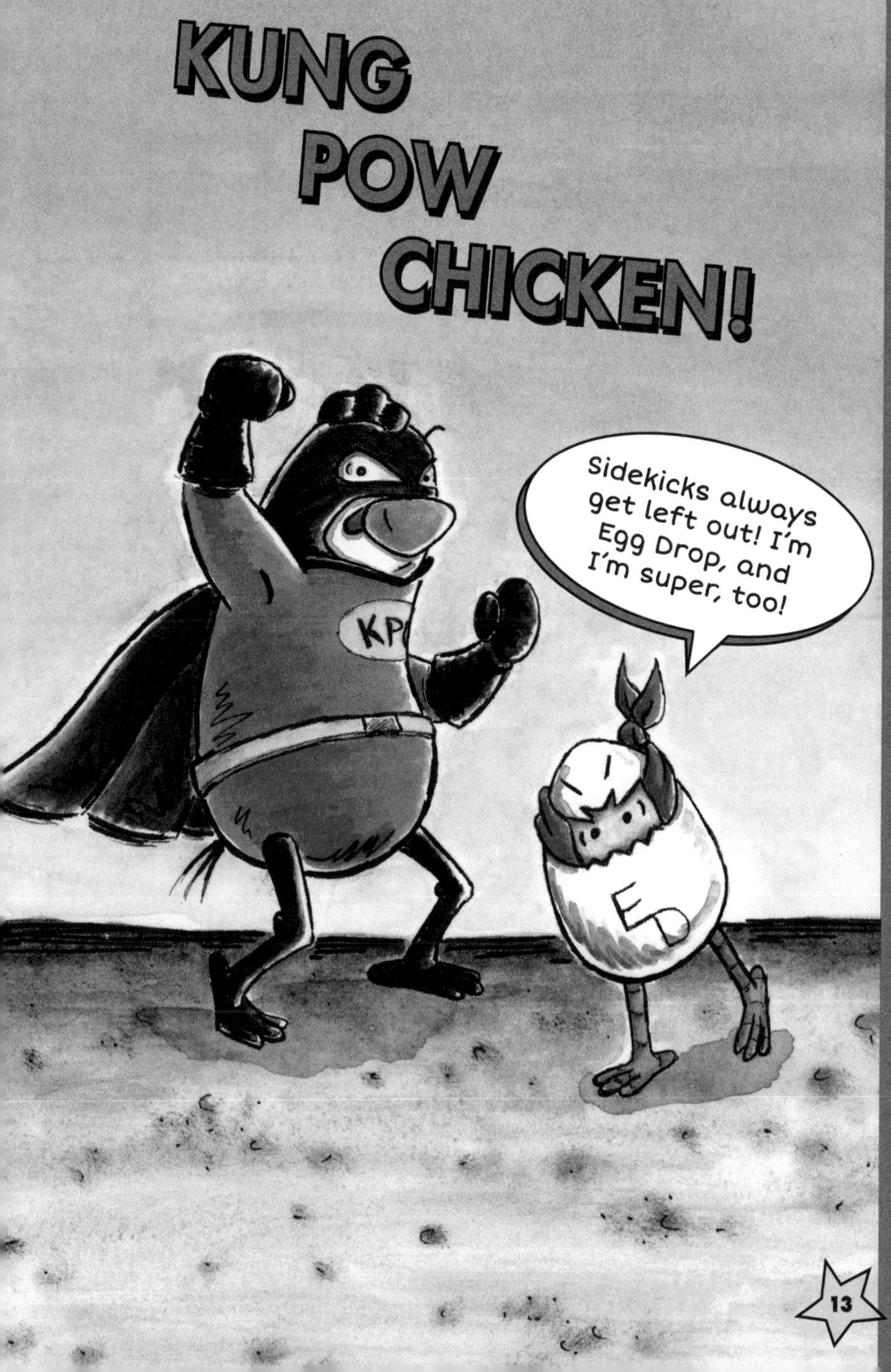
KUNG POW CHICKEN!
Sidekicks always get left out! I'm Egg Drop, and I'm super, too!
KP
ED

Gordon promised to use his powers to right wrongs, to fight bad guys, and to keep his room <u>super</u> clean.

superhero
promises

1. <u>be</u> super nice.
2. <u>be</u> super good.
3. <u>be</u> super tidy.

Egg Drop

Kung Pow Chicken

But Gordon hadn't met any bad guys yet. So he still had to do ordinary chicken things, like go to school.

Today was a bright fall day and Gordon was <u>super</u> excited about the school field trip to the Fowl Fall Festival.

Gordon's mother straightened his school tie
and handed him his lunch box.

Gordon carried his lunch box everywhere. But
he never let anyone see what was inside.

Mrs. Blue gave Gordon her very best mom stare. Gordon put on the hat.

Before her kids could escape, Mrs. Blue looped a scarf around Benny. Then she covered both Gordon and Benny in kisses.

Gordon and Benny walked to school.

When Gordon and Benny got to school, they joined their classmates out front. Everyone was excited to go to the Fowl Fall Festival.

Finally, the school bus arrived.

When they got to the festival, Gordon's teacher, Mr. Giblets, gave a long talk about rules.

Gordon and Benny were ready to burst. Gordon wanted to see the magician. Benny wanted to eat candy corn. And they both wanted to have a cookie.

Then Gordon's beak started to twitch. And his tail feathers began to wiggle.

Gordon could tell something was wrong, <u>very</u> wrong.

My birdy senses are tingling. . . . Someone must be up to no good!

Gordon and Benny pushed through the large flock of chickens. They were on the lookout for bad guys.

23

Suddenly, clucks and feathers filled the air. Gordon stared open-beaked. Everywhere he looked, feathers were blasting off chickens with a loud <u>POOF</u>!

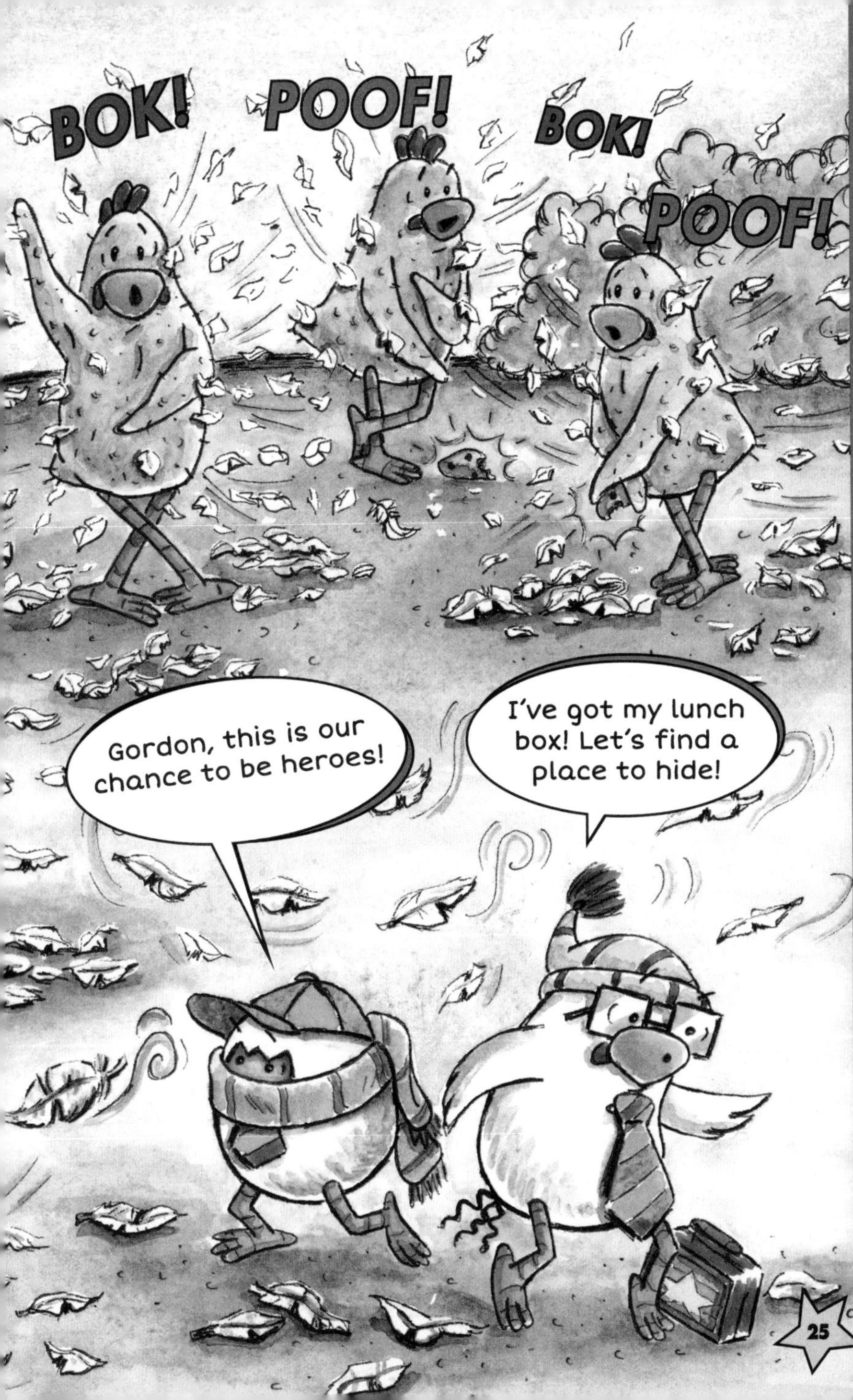
BOK!
POOF!
BOK!
POOF!
Gordon, this is our chance to be heroes!
I've got my lunch box! Let's find a place to hide!

They dashed inside. Gordon flung open his lunch box. . . .

A few seconds later, Kung Pow Chicken and his sidekick, Egg Drop, burst into action!

Kung Pow Chicken and Egg Drop searched for clues and talked to naked chickens.

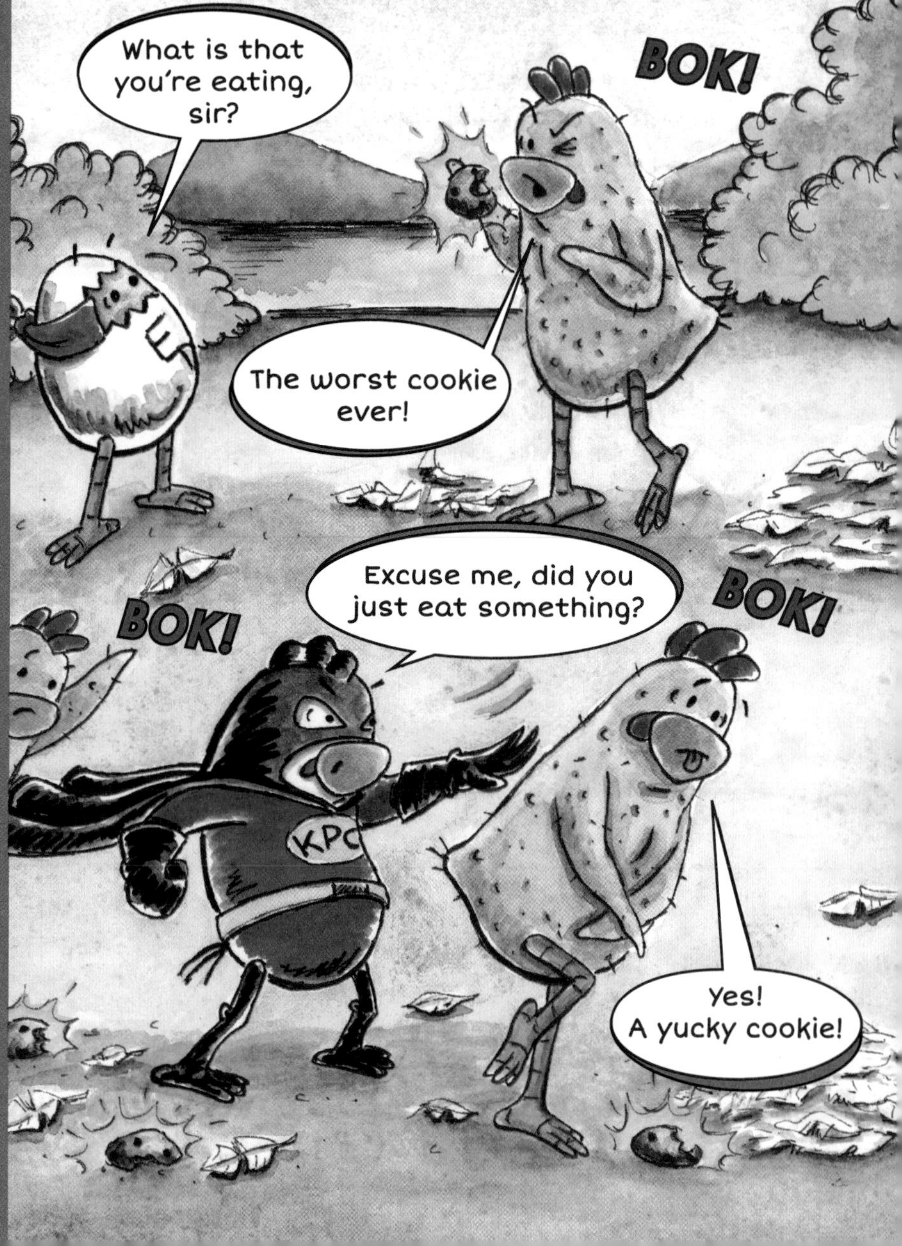
What is that you're eating, sir?
BOK!
The worst cookie ever!
BOK!
Excuse me, did you just eat something?
BOK!
KPC
Yes! A yucky cookie!

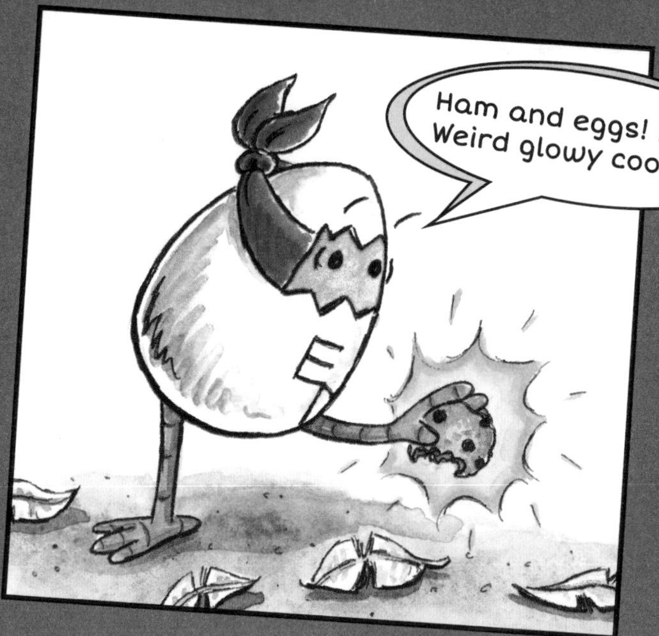
Ham and eggs! Look! Weird glowy cookies!

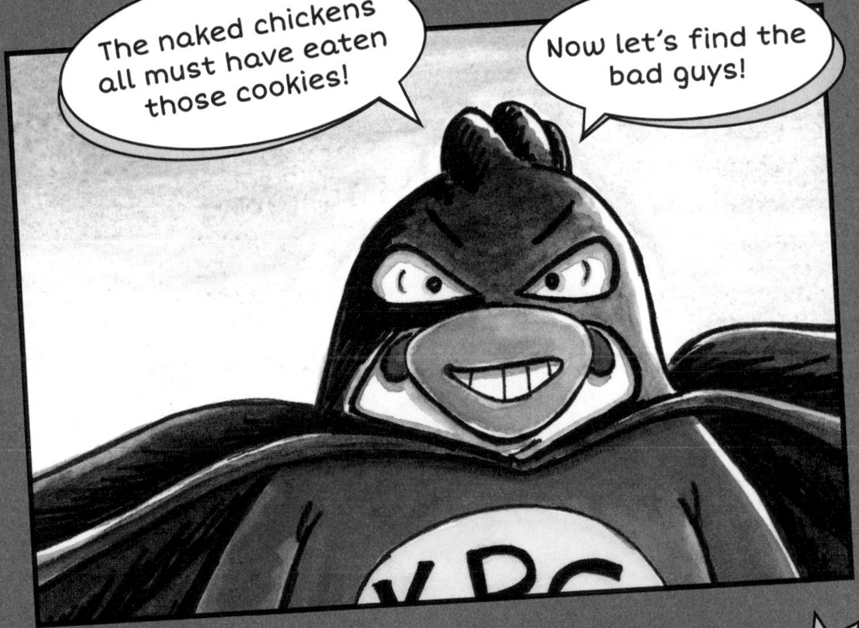
The naked chickens all must have eaten those cookies!
Now let's find the bad guys!

ITCH

ITCH

Granny Goosebumps's Warm Woolies

The heroes looked high and low for any sign of the bad guys. Then they spotted a busy booth selling hand-knit sweaters. Chilly naked chickens were scrambling to buy the sweaters.

My birdy senses are doing the Funky Chicken! That granny must be up to no good!

30

Kung Pow Chicken sneaked in for a
closer look.

But he was spotted!

Granny Goosebumps's Warm Woolies

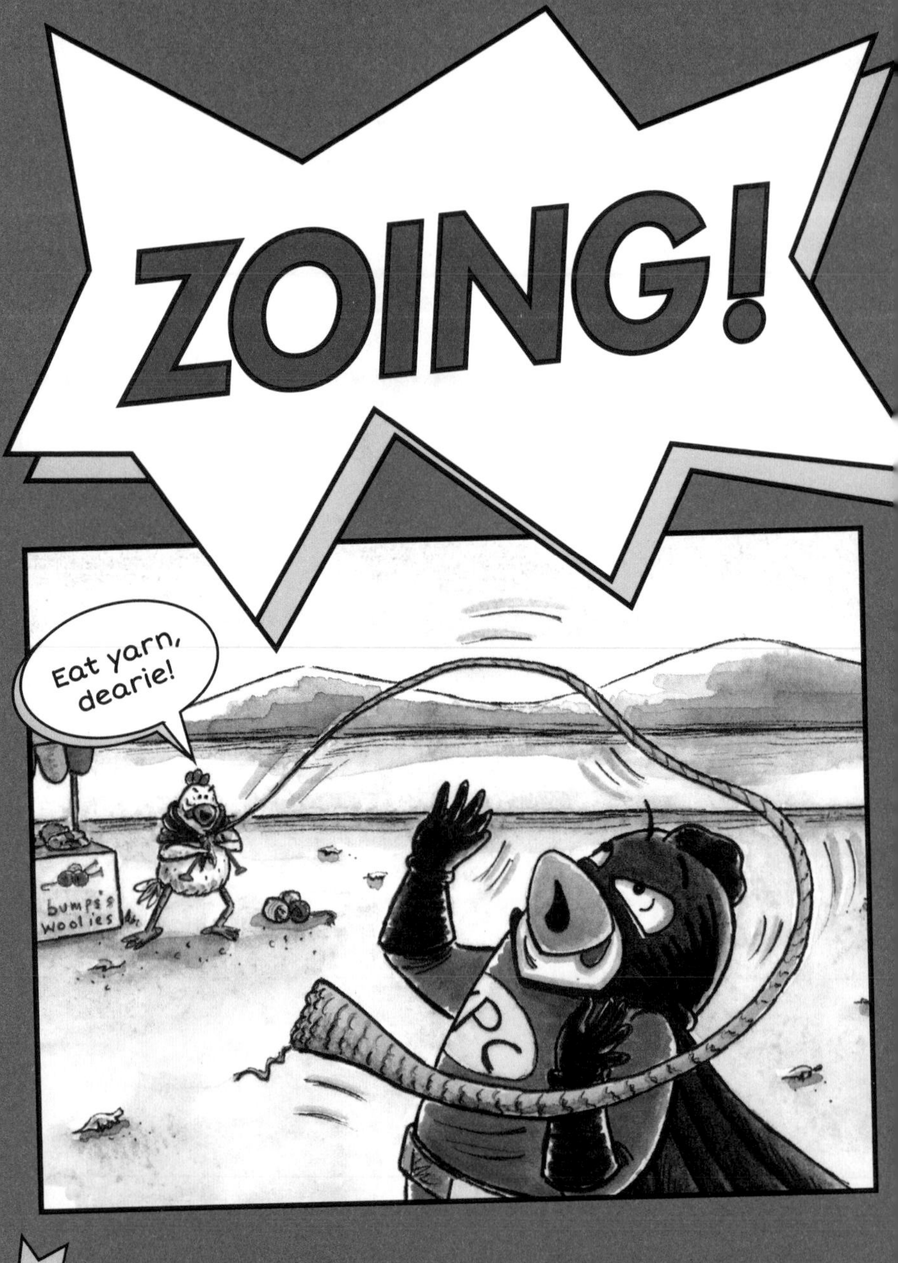
ZOING!
Eat yarn, dearie!
bumps's woolies
PC

Egg Drop stopped. He dropped. And he rolled like thunder. . . .

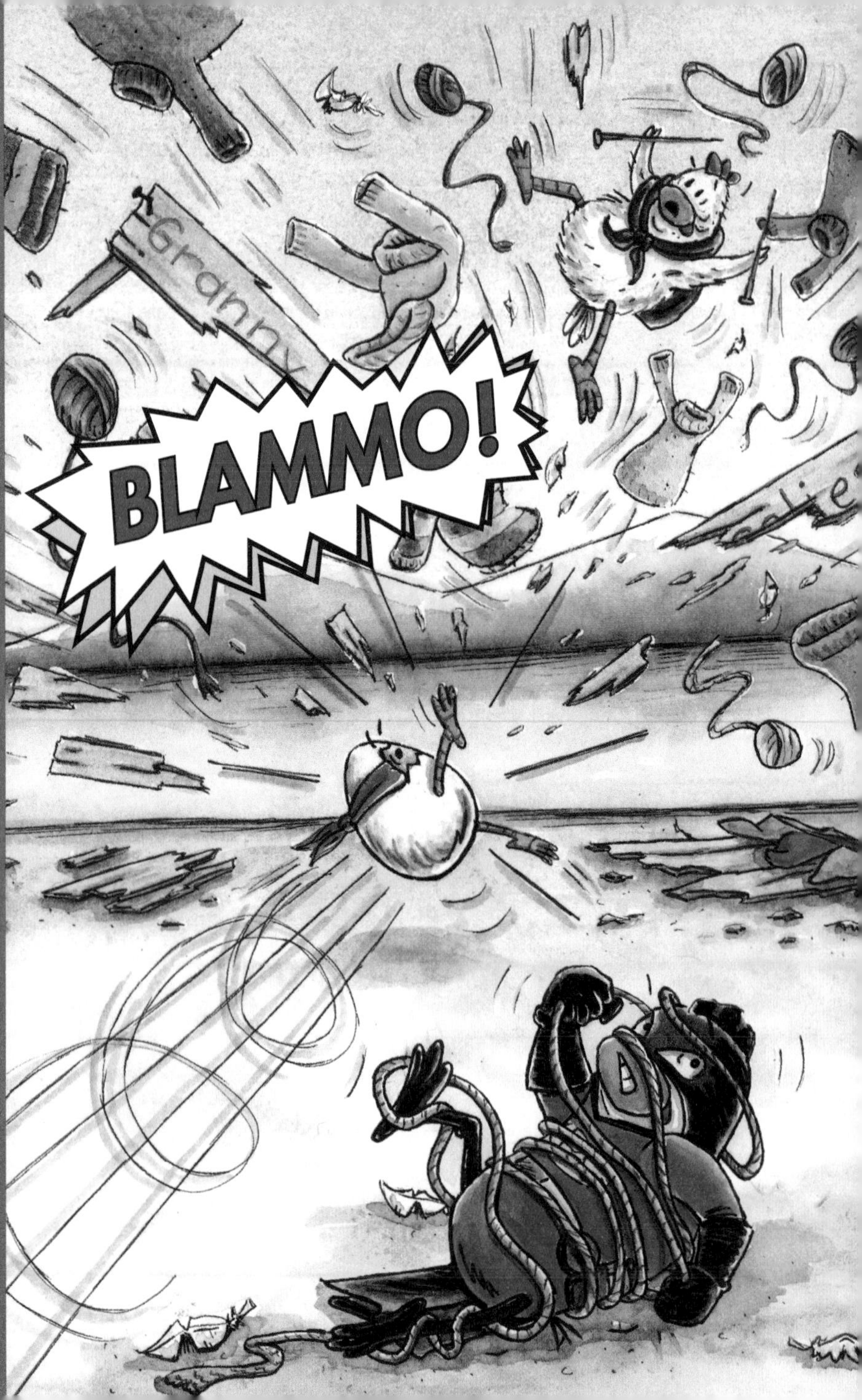
Granny
BLAMMO!

Kung Pow Chicken burst free of the tangled trap. He flashed his Drumsticks of Doom!

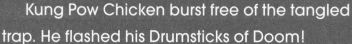

I'm Kung Pow Chicken! You are <u>doomed</u> to go to jail!

KAPOW!

I'm Granny Goosebumps! My Naughty Knitting Needles will have you in stitches!

Granny Goosebumps used her Naughty Knitting Needles to fling yarn at Kung Pow Chicken. He plucked the spinning yarn out of the air with his drumsticks. Then he became locked in a battle of knits with the grumpy granny.

PFFT!

KNIT!

Granny Goosebumps threw Kung Pow Chicken to the ground.

Suddenly, some other grannies came crashing through the crowd. They scooped up Granny Goosebumps and sped away!

Mwa-ha-ha!

So Granny Goosebumps isn't just selling sweaters! She's also selling those crummy cookies! But why? And why are those other grannies helping her?

Let's follow them, Kung Pow! . . . Hey, what's wrong?

I don't feel very super. I want to go home.

Gordon Hides Out

On the bus ride home, Gordon didn't want to talk. Outside, the city itched for a hero.

As soon as Gordon got home, he went straight to his room.

He put on his favorite bunny slippers.

He snuggled under his favorite blanket.

And he read his favorite comic book.

ROCKET ROOSTER #1

Benny knocked on Gordon's door.

Gordon knew Benny was right. He needed to be brave because the city needed his help. And no crummy cookie or grumpy granny was going to stop him. He grabbed his lunch box.

Gordon and Benny found their mother in the kitchen.

Gordon and Benny hopped on their Big Wheel. They rode up and down the streets. Every chicken they passed wore an itchy sweater and a sad face. Feathers and cookie crumbs covered the ground.

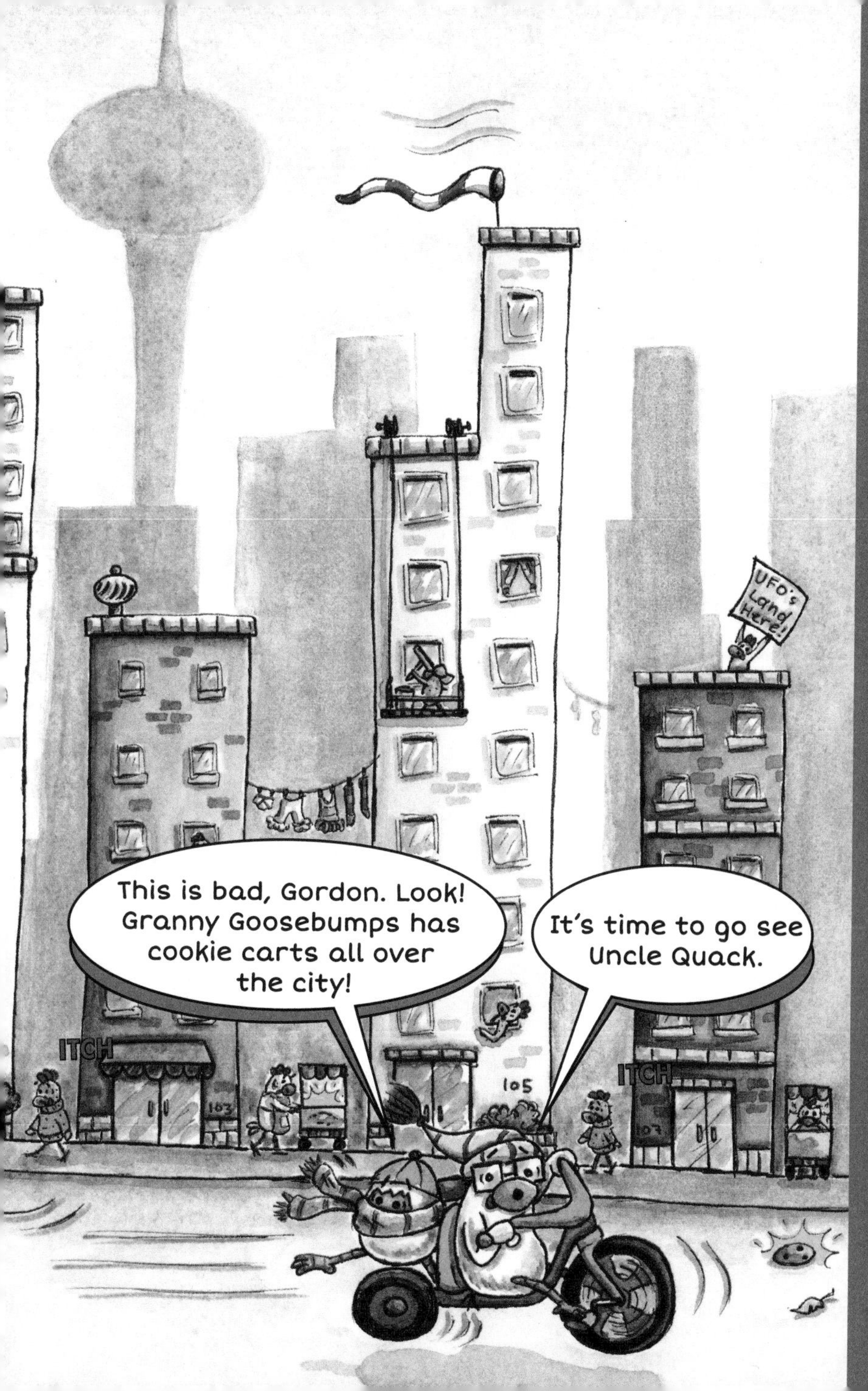

UFO's Land Here!
ITCH
103
105
ITCH
107
This is bad, Gordon. Look! Granny Goosebumps has cookie carts all over the city!
It's time to go see Uncle Quack.

Gordon handed Uncle Quack a cookie. Uncle Quack looked at it very carefully. He turned it over. He gave it a sniff.

Then Uncle Quack popped the cookie in his mouth.

Gordon told Uncle Quack all about Granny Goosebumps and what had happened at the Fowl Fall Festival.

Gordon and Benny ran to their Big Wheel.

Gordon and Benny zoomed away from the lab. They were headed back to the Fowl Fall Festival to look for clues. They <u>had</u> to find Granny Goosebumps.

Gordon and Benny parked the Big Wheel
under a tree. There wasn't a chicken in sight. So
Gordon let his birdy senses lead the way . . .

. . . and he fell flat on his face. Sometimes
Gordon's birdy senses were a pain in the beak.
When he opened his eyes, he spotted a clue!

Benny picked up the clue. He took a
closer look.

This card is the perfect clue! It has Granny Goosebumps's address on the back.

She must have dropped it during our battle!

Gordon and Benny ducked behind a bush. . . .

Kung Pow Chicken and Egg Drop jumped out, ready to kick Granny Goosebumps in the tail feathers!

LET'S GET CRACKING!

Kung Pow Chicken pressed a button on his Beak-Phone.

The Big Wheel turned into the Beak-Mobile. Kung Pow Chicken pedaled it at top speed.

The superheroes drove to the address on the card.

A granny in a pink housecoat and fuzzy slippers opened the door.

The granny went to get candies for the trick-or-treaters. While her back was turned, Kung Pow Chicken and Egg Drop ran past her and into the building.

Wait! She might have candy corn!

No time for snacks! Come on!

They tiptoed down empty hallway,
after empty hallway,
after empty hallway.

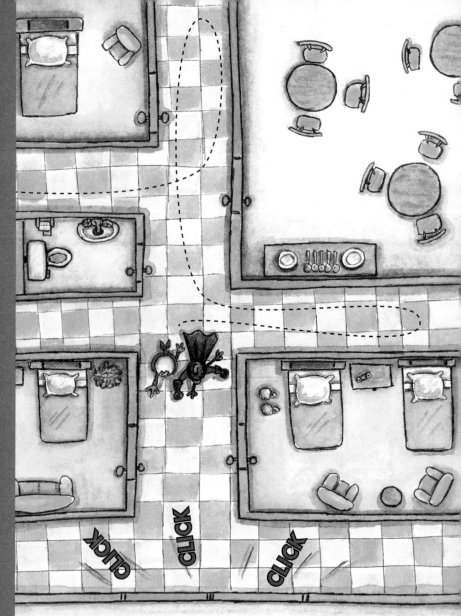

The emptiness was spooky. Finally, the heroes turned a corner and heard a scary sound.

Kung Pow Chicken gave Egg Drop a boost so he could peek inside.

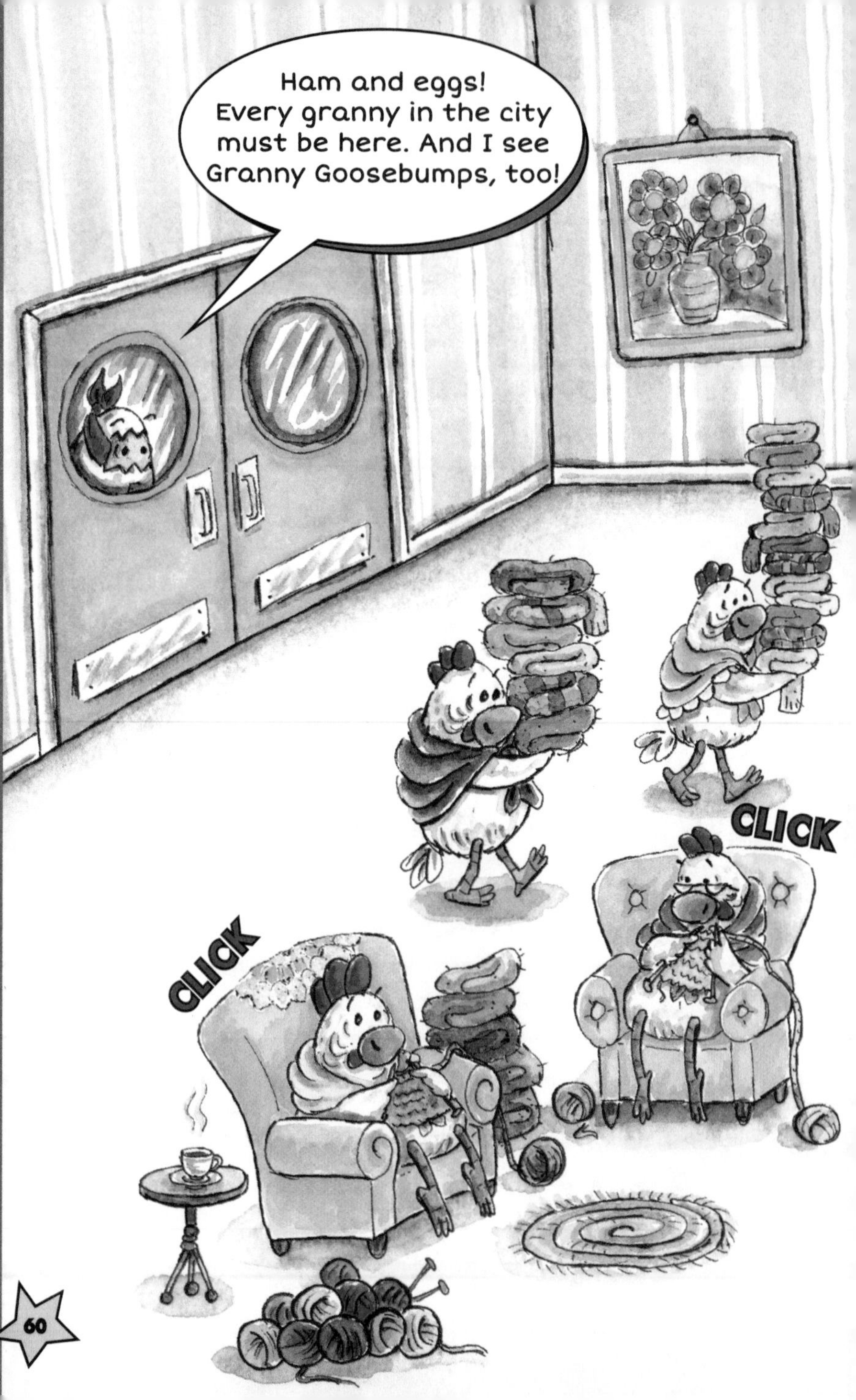
Ham and eggs! Every granny in the city must be here. And I see Granny Goosebumps, too!
CLICK
CLICK

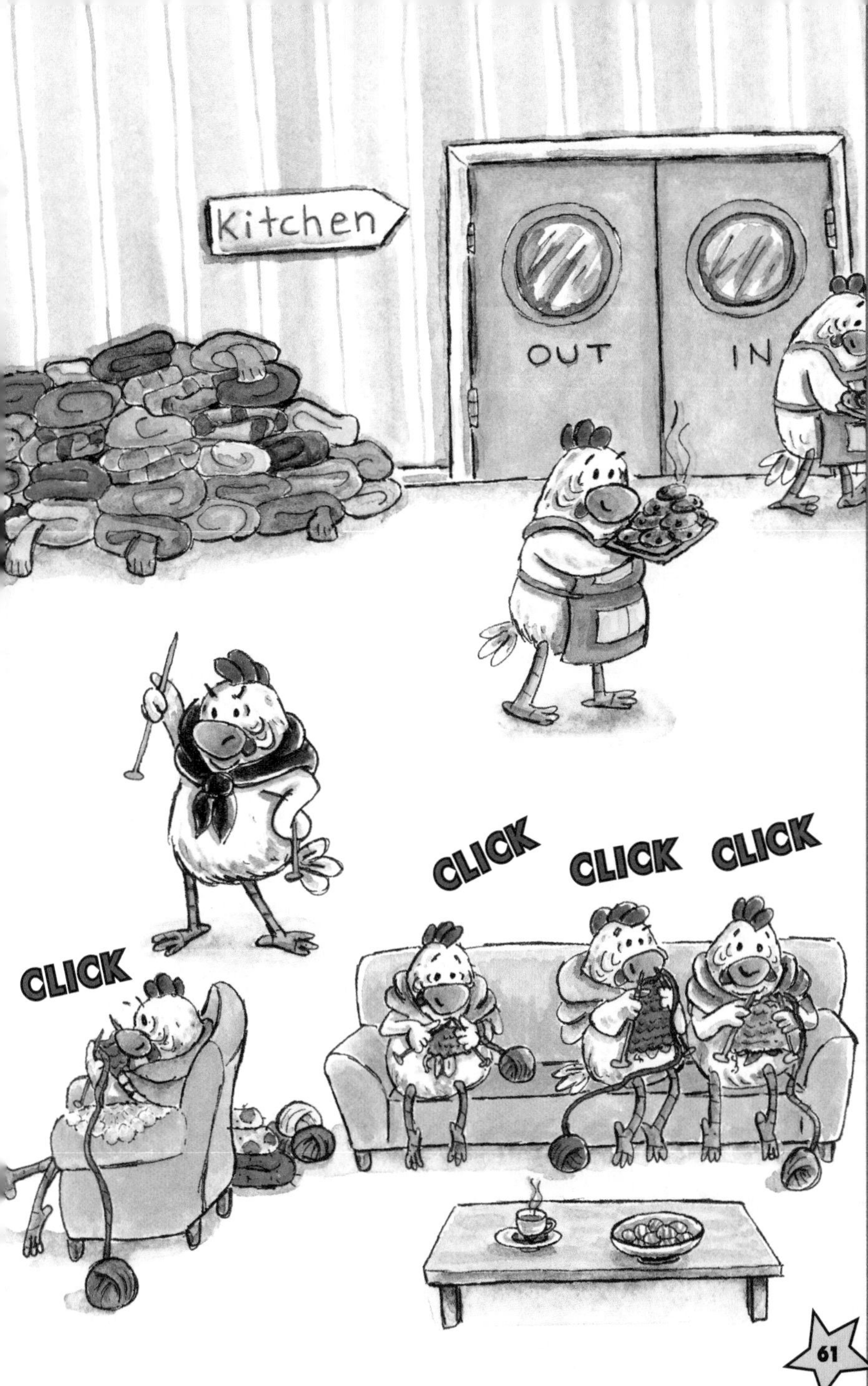
Kitchen
OUT
IN
CLICK
CLICK
CLICK
CLICK

Egg Drop leaned forward to get a better look. The door fell open. Kung Pow Chicken and Egg Drop both tumbled into the room.

Granny Goosebumps, you're one bad egg!

Thank you, dearie! Yes, soon my cookies will be all over the city. Every chicken will be naked and cold. They'll <u>need</u> to buy my sweaters! Then I'll have lots of money! And I can finally move to Florida!

Kung Pow Chicken and Egg Drop struggled and strained against the yarn. It was no use. They were wrapped up tight.

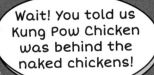

Wait! You told us Kung Pow Chicken was behind the naked chickens!

And you said the money you made would go to needy penguins!

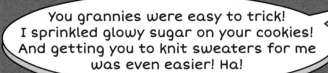

You grannies were easy to trick! I sprinkled glowy sugar on your cookies! And getting you to knit sweaters for me was even easier! Ha!

You'll never get away with this!

Want to bet your feathers? Now take a bite of this cookie!

Kung Pow Chicken's beak trembled. He shrank away from the glowing cookie. Then the Beak-Phone rang.

RIINNG! ♫ ♪

Kung Pow Chicken squiggled under the yarn. He popped his phone through the strands. It was his mother calling.

You boys are late for dinner! You are both in BIG trouble!!

That did it. Granny Goosebumps had made Kung Pow Chicken late for dinner. He was mad! It was time to show this bad granny who wore the leotard. It was time to be a superhero. He sucked in a super breath and —

BOK!

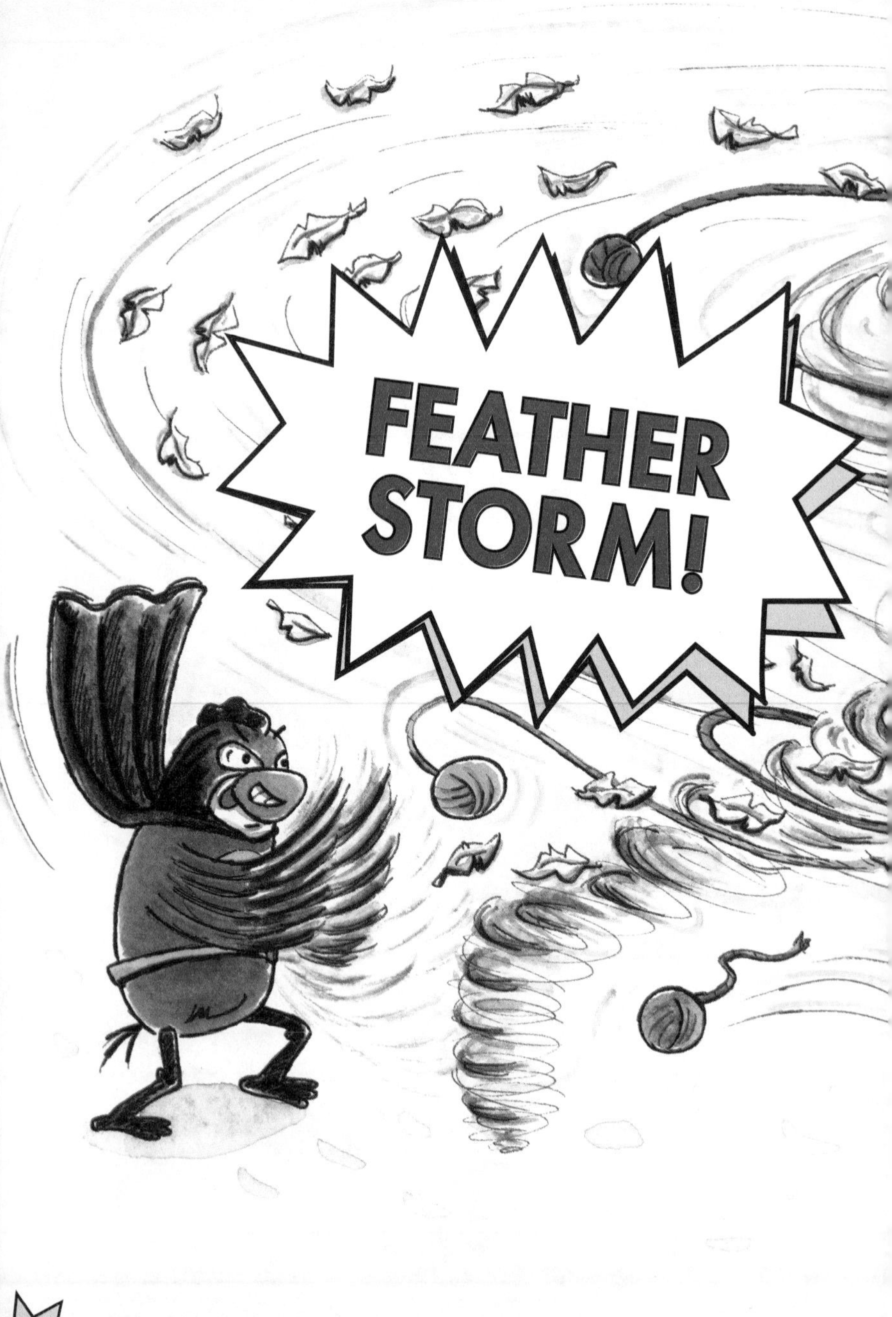
FEATHER STORM!

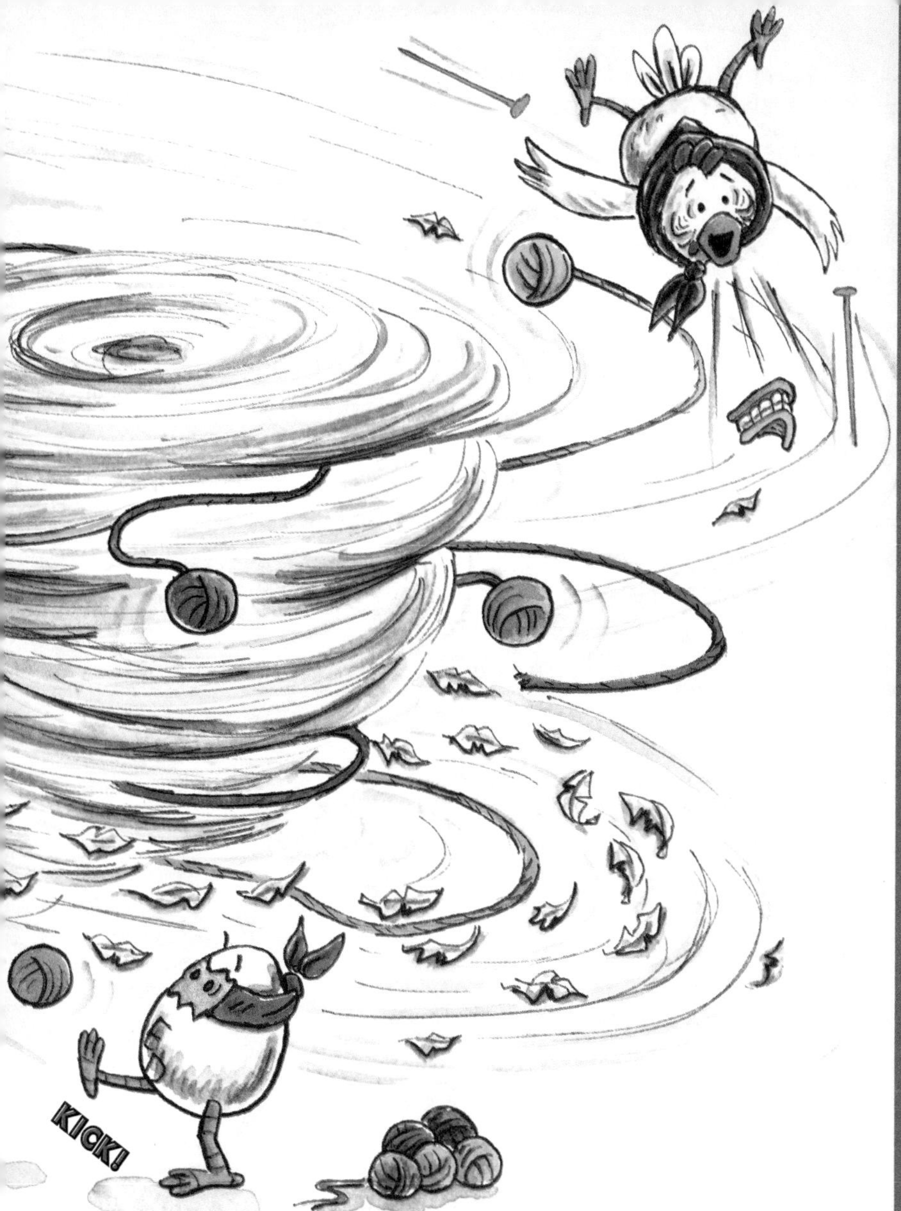
KICK!

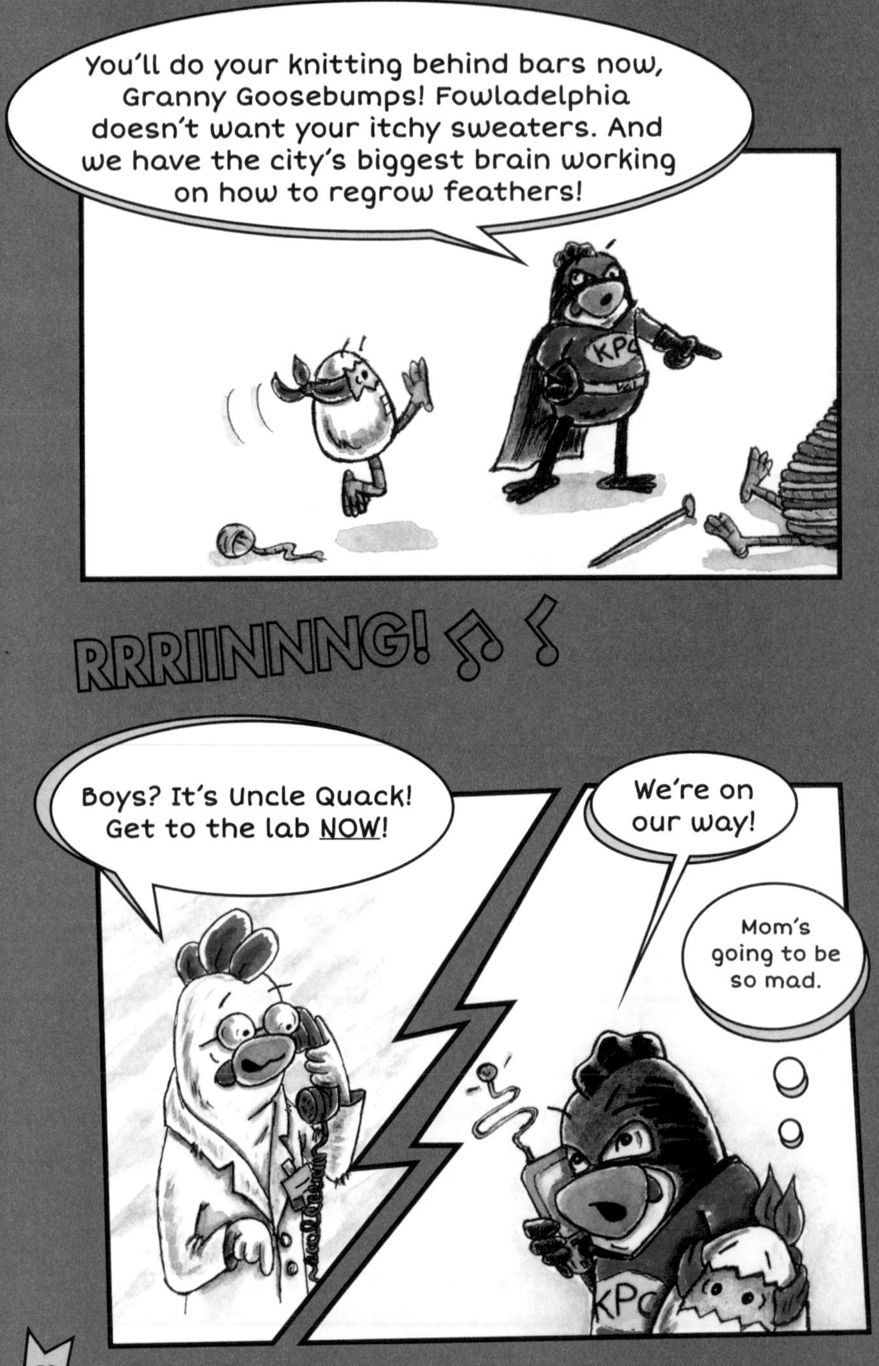
You'll do your knitting behind bars now, Granny Goosebumps! Fowladelphia doesn't want your itchy sweaters. And we have the city's biggest brain working on how to regrow feathers!
RRRIINNNG!
Boys? It's Uncle Quack! Get to the lab NOW!
We're on our way!
Mom's going to be so mad.

Uncle Quack had created a glowy milk. He had dunked himself in it and now his feathers were back fuller than ever! But he didn't know how to get the milk to all the other naked chickens.

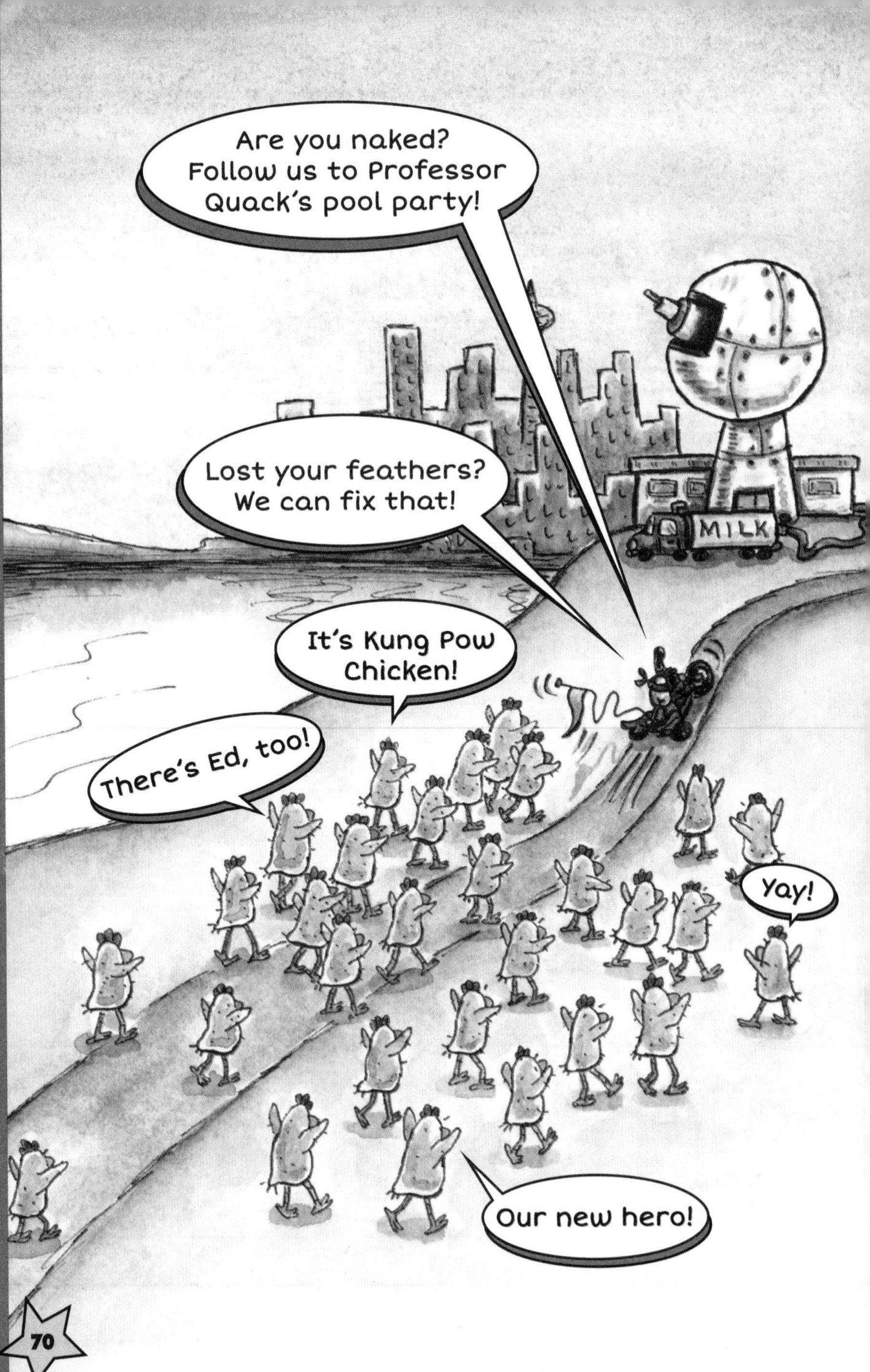
Are you naked? Follow us to Professor Quack's pool party!
Lost your feathers? We can fix that!
MILK
It's Kung Pow Chicken!
There's Ed, too!
Yay!
Our new hero!

Granny Goosebumps had been caught, and the naked chickens were about to regrow their feathers. Kung Pow Chicken and Egg Drop could be ordinary chickens again.

Benny, I'm stuck! Help me get this leotard off!

Whose idea was it for superheroes to wear leotards, anyway?

Gordon and Benny joined Uncle Quack's pool party. Soon, all of the naked chickens had been dunked in the pool of glowy milk. They showed off their fine new feathers.

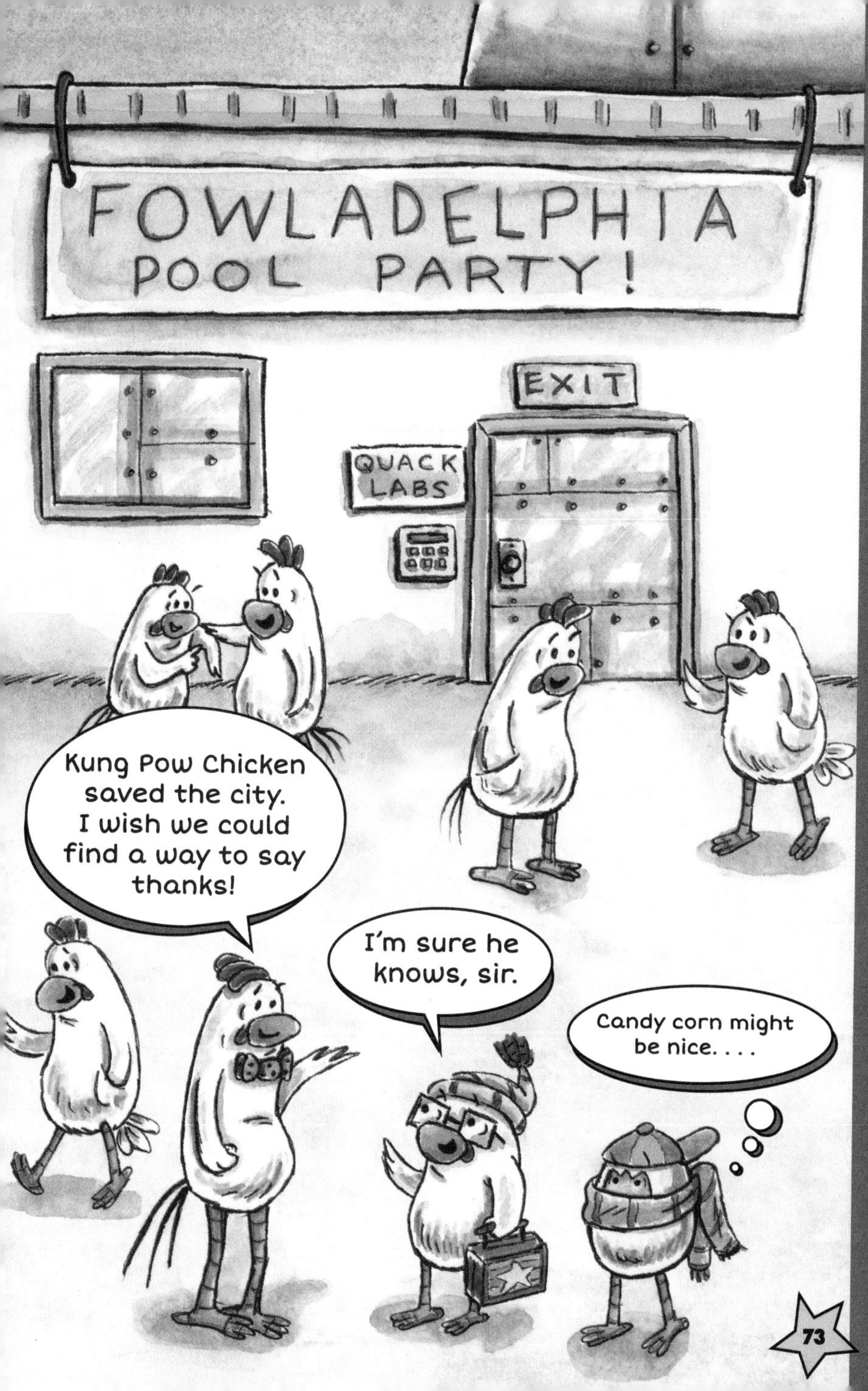
FOWLADELPHIA POOL PARTY!
EXIT
QUACK LABS
Kung Pow Chicken saved the city. I wish we could find a way to say thanks!
I'm sure he knows, sir.
Candy corn might be nice. . . .

Gordon and Benny rode home as fast as
Gordon's chicken legs could go.
Mrs. Blue met them at the door.

Gordon and Benedict Blue! I should take away your Big Wheel!

But Uncle Quack called and said you had dinner at the lab. And he said you helped those poor naked chickens I saw on the news!

<u>So</u> you're not in trouble. But next time, you had better call me!

We will, Mom.

Hmmph. It's not <u>my</u> fault. I can't even have a phone!

Then she gave them both a kiss and sent
them off to bed.

Gordon and Benny sat on Gordon's bed. They talked about everything that had happened that day. Gordon was proud to finally be a <u>real</u> superhero.

Suddenly, Gordon's tail feathers began to wiggle.

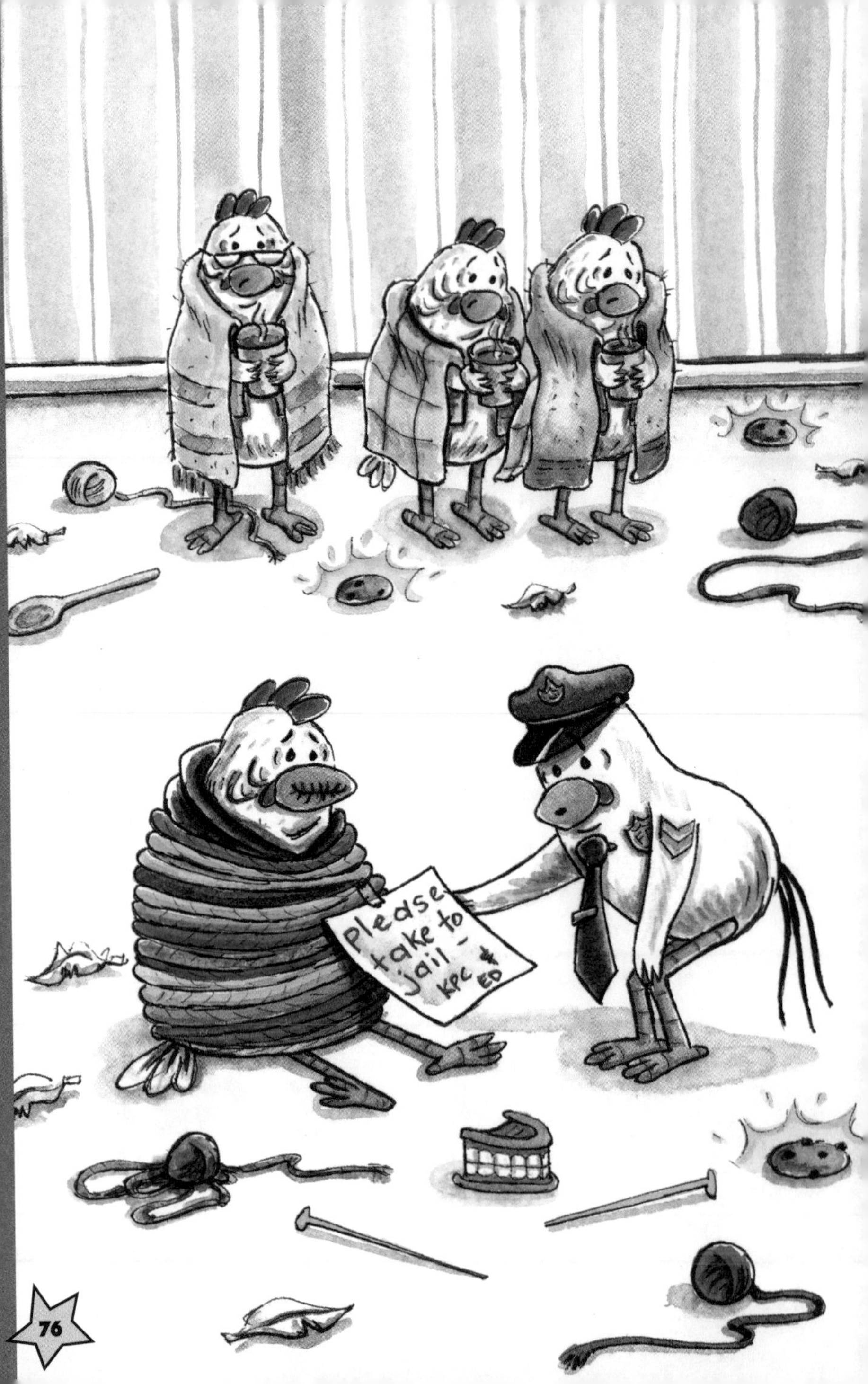
Please
take to
jail
KPC
&
ED

KUNG POW CHICKEN ★

PROVE YOUR SUPERHERO KNOW-HOW!

How did Gordon and Benny get superpowers?

How does Gordon know when danger is near?

What is Granny Goosebumps's evil plan? And how do Gordon and Benny save the day?

How is Kung Pow Chicken similar to superheroes in other stories?

Give yourself a superhero name, draw your costume, and write about why <u>you</u> want to be a superhero.

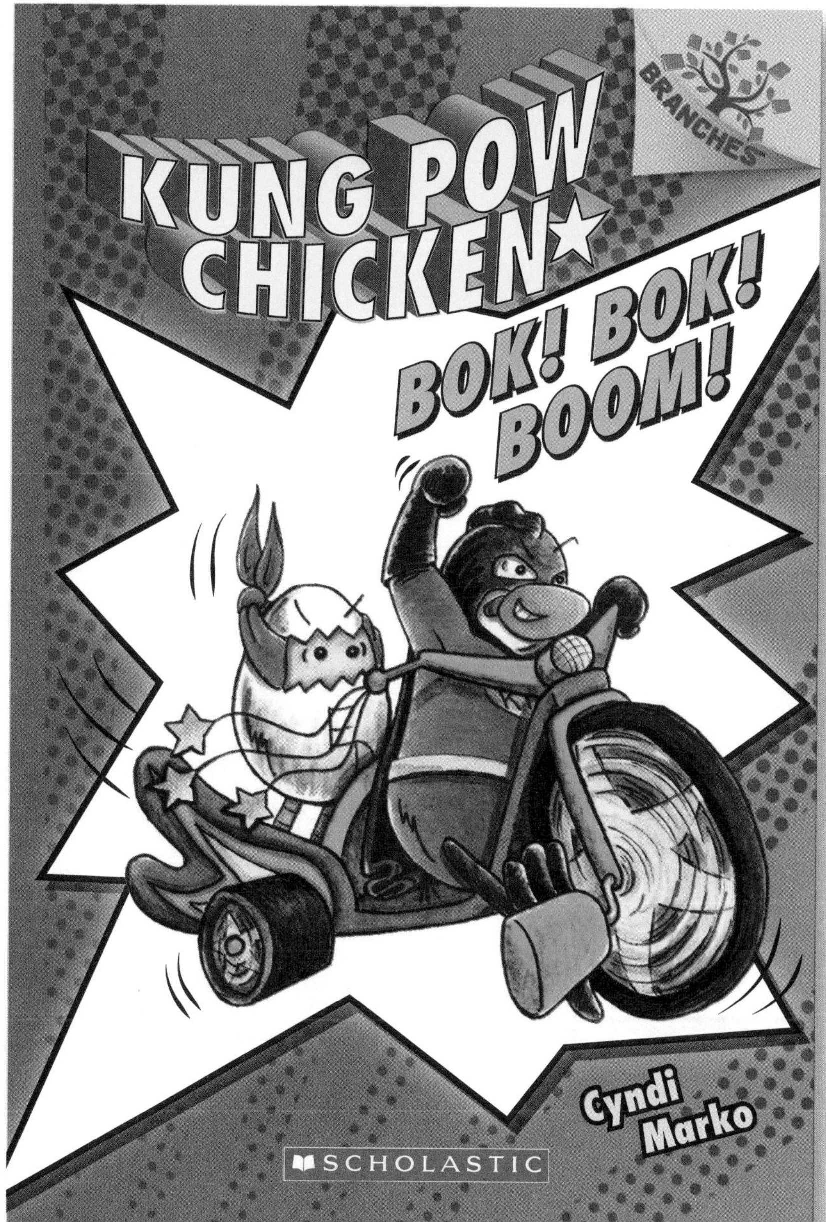
BRANCHES
KUNG POW CHICKEN
BOK! BOK! BOOM!
Cyndi Marko
SCHOLASTIC

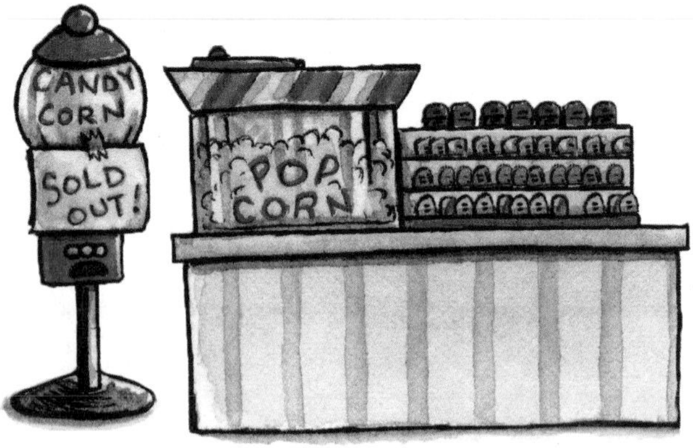
CANDY CORN
SOLD OUT!
POP CORN

TABLE OF CONTENTS

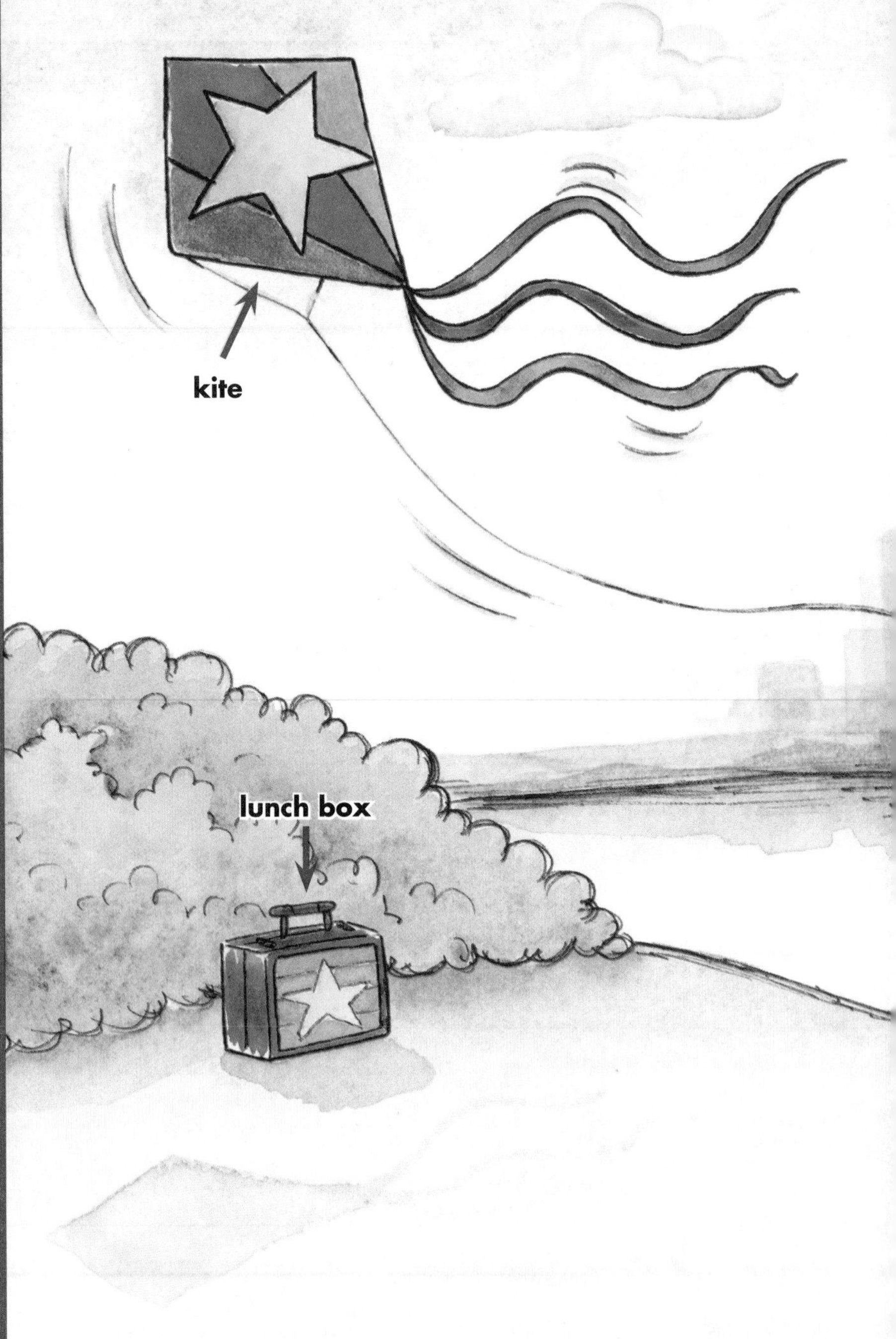
kite
lunch box

Super Chicken

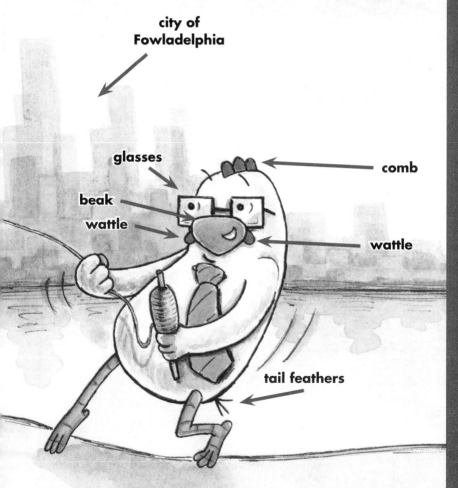

city of Fowladelphia

glasses

comb

beak

wattle

wattle

tail feathers

Gordon Blue seemed like an ordinary chicken.

He was in second grade at an ordinary
school in the ordinary city of Fowladelphia.

And he had an ordinary family. (Sort of.)

But Gordon had a <u>super</u> secret.

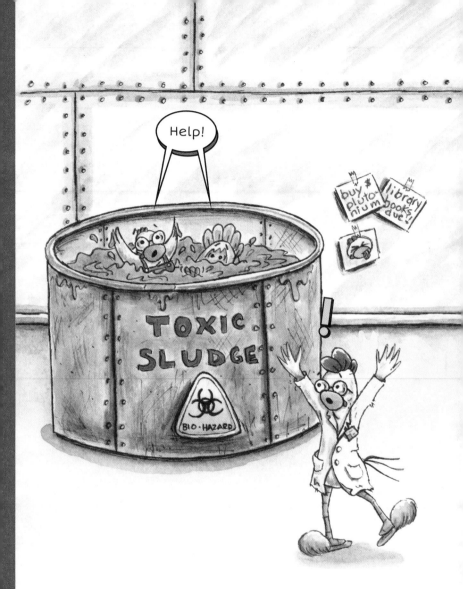

When Gordon was younger, he and Benny
fell into a vat of toxic sludge at their Uncle
Quack's lab.

The toxic sludge was no ordinary toxic sludge. It had given Gordon superpowers.

Gordon promised only to use his superpowers for good.

Uncle Quack had promised to keep Gordon's secret. But it was still <u>super</u> tricky to keep the secret from Gordon's mom.

Gordon had a super suit. He kept it hidden in his lunch box. And he carried his lunch box everywhere. Whenever he squeezed into his super suit, he became Kung Pow Chicken.

Last week, Kung Pow Chicken had saved the chickens of Fowladelphia from a bad guy called Granny Goosebumps.

THE FOWL

HOODED HERO SAVES CITY

A new hero, Kung Pow Chicken, stopped bad guy Granny Goosebumps. The grumpy granny sold glowy cookies that made many chickens lose their feathers. Then the granny sold sweaters to those birds-in-the-buff! Kung Pow Chicken beat Granny Goosebumps in a battle. And Professor Quack Blue made a glowy milk to regrow the naked chickens' feathers. Now the granny does her knitting in jail.

When asked for a comment, Granny Goosebumps said, "I wish I were in Florida."

TIMES

FAMOUS SINGER IN TOWN

Miss Honey Comb is well-known for her super-high singing voice. She will be singing at the Fowladelphia Opera House. Get tickets today!

BIG-SHOT SOUND SCIENTIST IS BACK

Dr. Screech grew up in Fowladelphia, and has returned to the city this week. Dr. Screech said he plans to go to the opera. And he said he might like to see what's shaking at the Public Library, too.

Now Kung Pow Chicken was totally famous.
But being a famous superhero wasn't easy.

Gordon couldn't
tell any of his friends
his <u>super</u> secret.

You're
grounded!

Fighting bad
guys sometimes
made him late
for dinner.

And a snoopy
reporter named
Sam Snood just
never got his
story right.

HELPFUL HERO
OR TROUBLE
IN TIGHTS?

Sam Snood
Junior
Reporter

Kung Pow Chicken may
wear a super suit, but he
has super-bad manners. He
is rude to grown-ups — just
ask Granny Goosebumps!

There is a reward if you can
tell me Kung Pow Chicken's
real name!

$$REWARD$$

Tonight, Gordon would have to be just an ordinary chicken. He had to go with his family to the <u>la-dee-da</u> opera to hear overstuffed chickens sing.

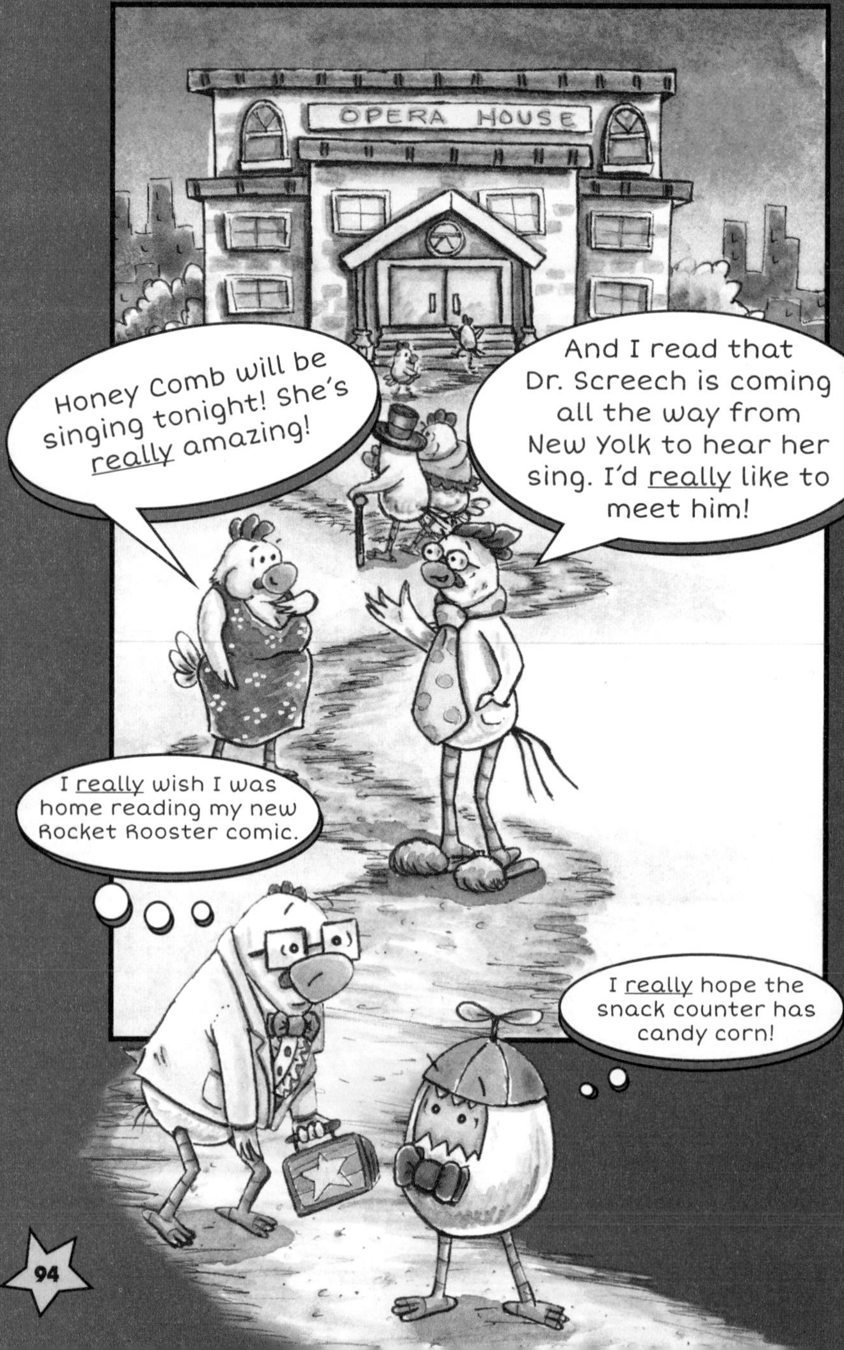
OPERA HOUSE
Honey Comb will be singing tonight! She's really amazing!
And I read that Dr. Screech is coming all the way from New Yolk to hear her sing. I'd really like to meet him!
I really wish I was home reading my new Rocket Rooster comic.
I really hope the snack counter has candy corn!

The Fat Lady Sings **2**

SQUAAAAAAAAAAK!

Honey Comb sang and sang. But Gordon had no clue what she was singing about.

Gordon didn't like the opera. He had never been so bored in his whole life. Then he spotted Sam Snood.

Honey Comb had been singing <u>forever</u>.
At last, the curtain dropped and the singing
stopped.

Yay! It's over!

This is just a quick
break to grab a
snack, Gordie. We'll
get to hear more
singing after!

Mrs. Blue went to the snack counter. Uncle Quack, Gordon, and Benny were waiting for her when a strange chicken walked over. A <u>very</u> strange chicken.

Then Dr. Screech said he had to go back to his seat. Gordon's tail feathers began to wiggle.

Gordon and Benny looked around. They didn't see anything out of the ordinary.

Then Mrs. Blue said it was time to go back to their seats. Soon, Honey Comb was singing again. Gordon's tail feathers were still wiggling, but everything seemed fine.

Suddenly a giant hook came down. It snagged Honey Comb, yanking her up into the air.

Gordon's birdy senses almost shook him
out of his seat. Mrs. Blue fainted. Uncle Quack
caught her just in time.

Uncle Quack,
Honey Comb has
been <u>chicknapped</u>!
My birdy senses are
going bananas!

This city needs a
hero! Get to work,
boys! I'll stay with
your mom!

Look! That hook
came from
the roof!

Bad guys needed catching. A chicken
needed saving. Gordon grabbed his lunch box.
Then he and Benny looked for a place to hide.

Gordon and Benny changed into their super suits.
Now Kung Pow Chicken and Egg Drop were
ready to get cracking.

The superheroes quickly climbed up a ladder to the roof. They peeked out. Honey Comb was still dangling from the hook. And the hook was dangling from a giant crane arm. Dr. Screech sat at the controls!

SQUAAAAWK! Help!

TRAPDOOR

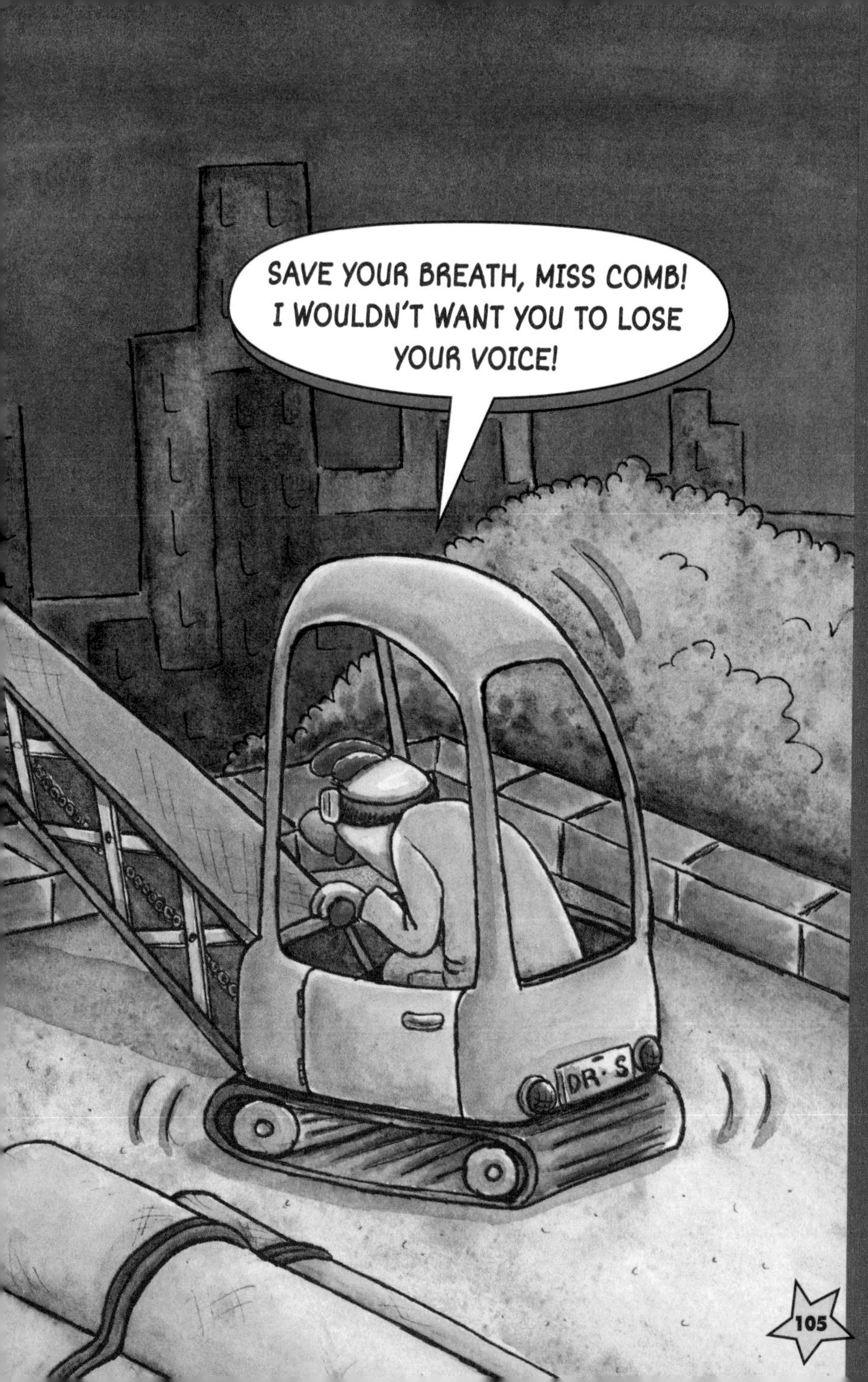
SAVE YOUR BREATH, MISS COMB! I WOULDN'T WANT YOU TO LOSE YOUR VOICE!
DR·S

Kung Pow Chicken and Egg Drop ducked back down.

I can't believe Dr. Screech is the bad guy!

I can't believe anyone would want to chicknap that singing lady!

Then Kung Pow Chicken took a deep breath. He jumped out onto the roof. He was ready to kick Dr. Screech in the wattles.

Help! No arms!

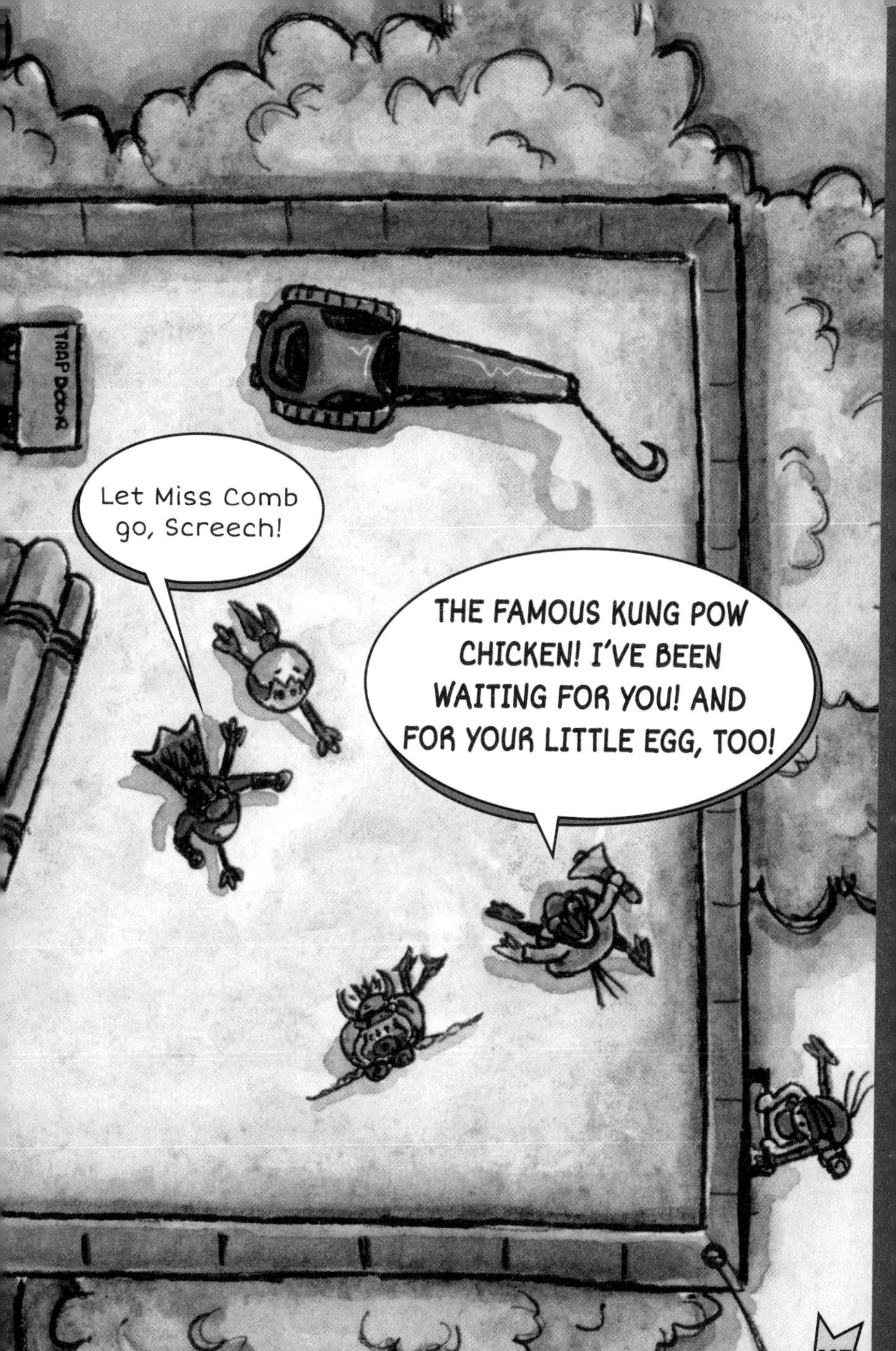
TRAP DOOR
Let Miss Comb go, Screech!
THE FAMOUS KUNG POW CHICKEN! I'VE BEEN WAITING FOR YOU! AND FOR YOUR LITTLE EGG, TOO!

Dr. Screech held a funny-looking cone up to his beak. It was a megaphone and it made everything he said <u>mega</u> loud.

MY MEGA-MEGAPHONE MAKES MY VOICE MEGA LOUD. IT ALSO FLINGS MEGA TRAPS!

SQUAWK!

The heroes were trapped!

Kung Pow Chicken used his Power Peck to break free. But it was too late.

Dr. Screech slung Honey Comb over his shoulder. Then he zipped away.

Come on! After them!

Kung Pow, stop! You'll slip and fall!

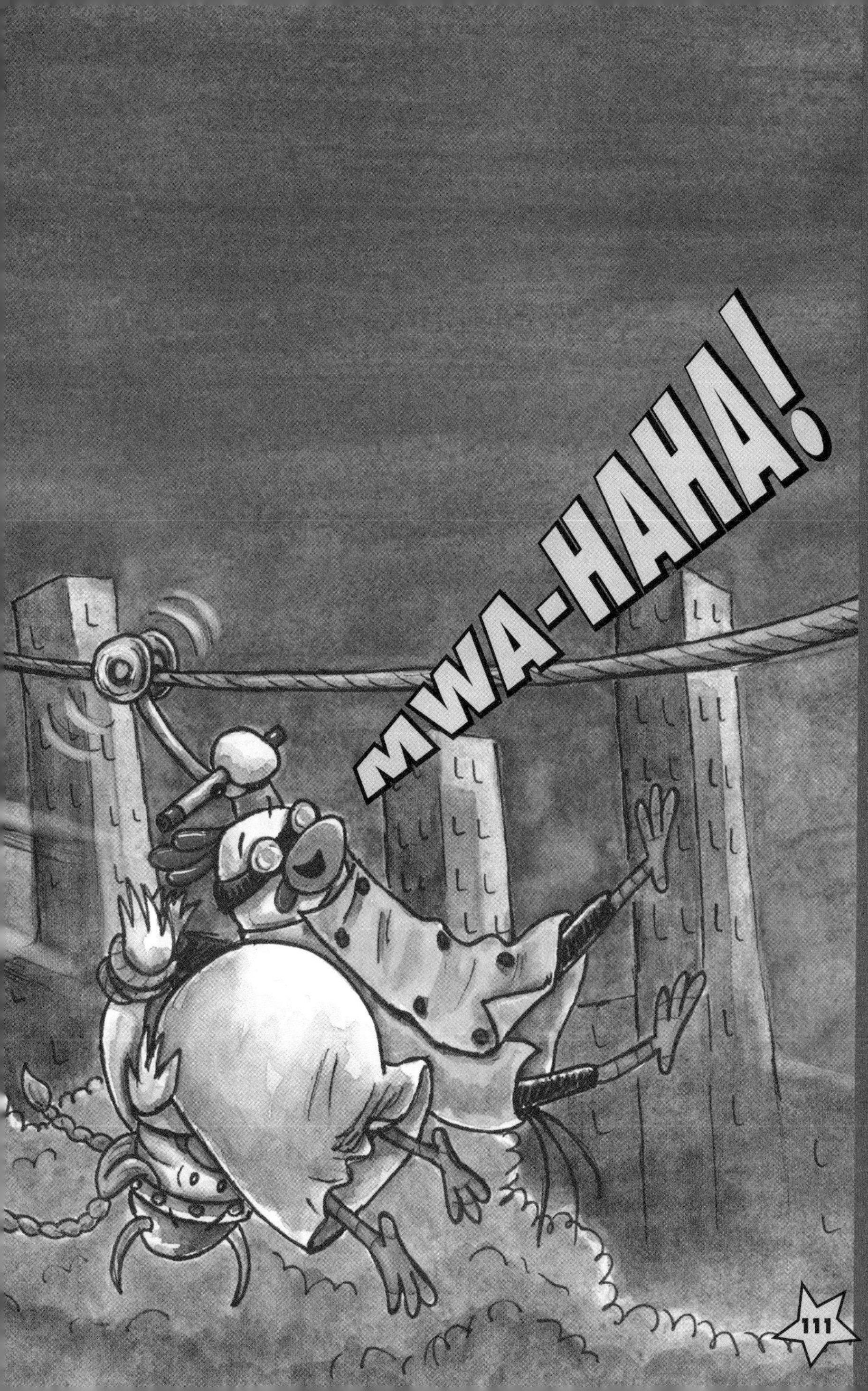
MWA-HAHA!

RIINNG!

Kung Pow Chicken's Beak-Phone was ringing.
It was Uncle Quack.

Boys, your mom is awake! She wants to know where you are! Come back! Quick!

But what about Honey Comb?

We'll have to follow Dr. Screech later. Come on!

Kung Pow Chicken and Egg Drop climbed down from the roof. Then they changed back into their fancy clothes.

They found their mom by the snack counter. That reporter Sam Snood was asking her some questions.

Gordon quickly filled Uncle Quack in on what had happened on the roof.

Sound is made of waves. If you can make a loud enough noise, then the sound waves can shake things to pieces.

Ham and eggs! Honey Comb was voted the loudest singer five years in a row! Dr. Screech could use her voice to shake the city to bits!

Uncle, can you make <u>anything</u> to help us? We need to follow Screech. And that zip line is our only clue!

Just then, Mrs. Blue marched over to where the boys were talking with Uncle Quack.

Mrs. Blue gave Gordon and Benny kisses.
Then she sent them off with their Uncle Quack.

As soon as they got to the lab, Gordon and Benny put on their super suits. Uncle Quack gave them a gadget to help them follow Dr. Screech's zip line.

Kung Pow Chicken took out his phone. He pressed the AUTO-BEAK button to make the Beak-Mobile come to the lab.

Then he pedaled back to the opera house to pick up Dr. Screech's trail.

The opera house looked dark and empty—and locked. Kung Pow Chicken and Egg Drop crept around the building. They looked for a way up to the roof.

I don't see a way up. Do you?

No. Maybe on the other side?

They started to climb up the waterspout. But Kung Pow Chicken saw an itsy-bitsy spider.

Kung Pow Chicken flung the Beak-A-Rang up to the roof. Then he and Benny started climbing.

Boy, this is hard work!

At least you have arms!

PUFF PUFF

Finally, they reached the roof.

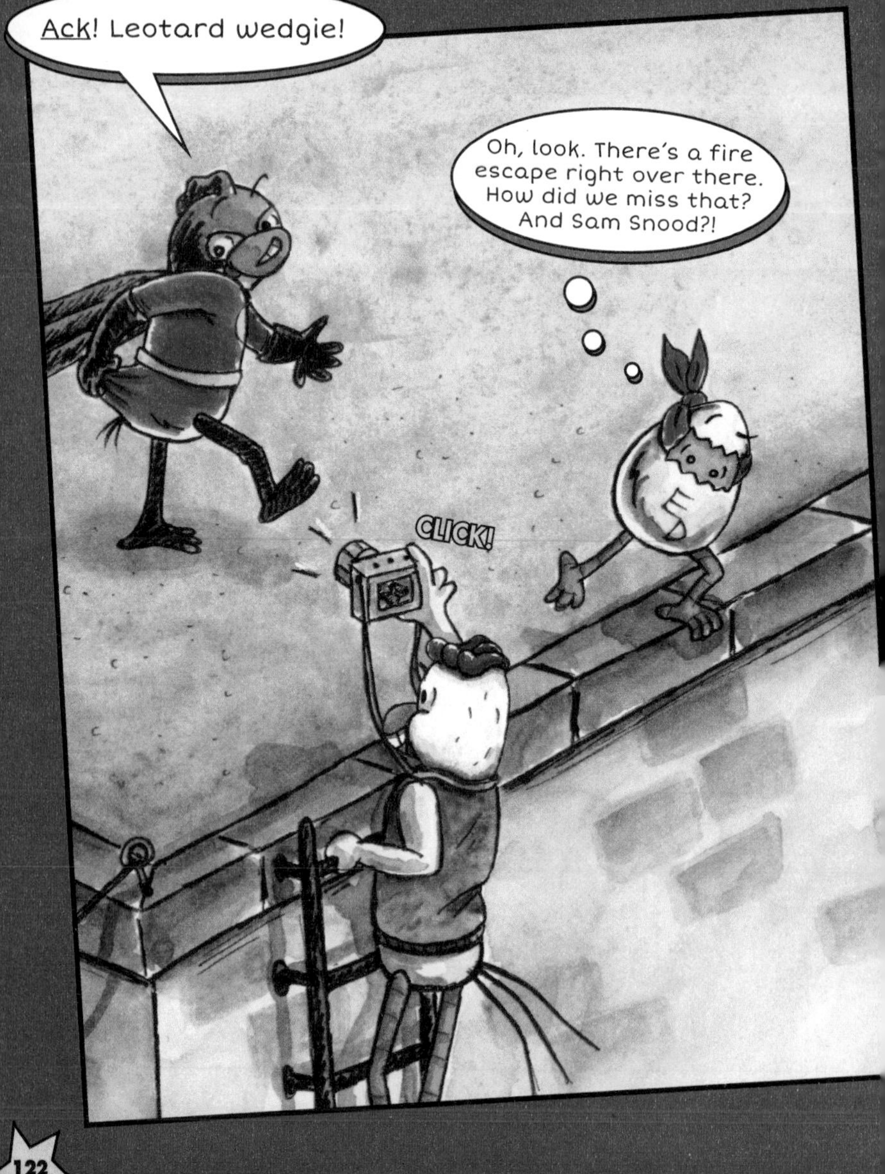
Ack! Leotard wedgie!
Oh, look. There's a fire escape right over there. How did we miss that? And Sam Snood?!
CLICK!

Kung Pow Chicken thought Sam Snood was a real pain in the beak. But he did not have time to talk to Sam Snood now. There was a bad guy on the loose.

Kung Pow Chicken hung Uncle Quack's gadget over the zip line. Then, with Egg Drop holding on tight, he zipped!

The heroes zipped
      past many streets,
            and over many rooftops,
                  until they came to
                        the end of the line.

Dr. Screech was there waiting for them. He squawked into his Mega-Megaphone. The loud mega sound waves blasted Kung Pow Chicken and Egg Drop right off the roof.

Kung Pow Chicken flung the Beak-A-Rang.
He caught Egg Drop just in time!

Kung Pow Chicken was no birdbrain. He knew what to do. He sucked in a super breath and—

Dr. Screech was blown backward off of the rooftop. But he flung his arms and legs out wide.

Dr. Screech was wearing a flight suit!

Then Dr. Screech flew away.

Kung Pow Chicken slid to the ground. He was beat. <u>He</u> couldn't fly like Dr. Screech. Kung Pow Chicken zipped the Beak-A-Rang into his belt.

The sleepy heroes were ready to go home. Kung Pow Chicken pressed the AUTO-BEAK button on his Beak-Phone. The Beak-Mobile pulled up.

Gordon Gets His Wings

Gordon took a quick power nap when he got home. He woke up feeling like a new chicken. But while he was eating breakfast, he saw the front page of his mom's newspaper. . . .

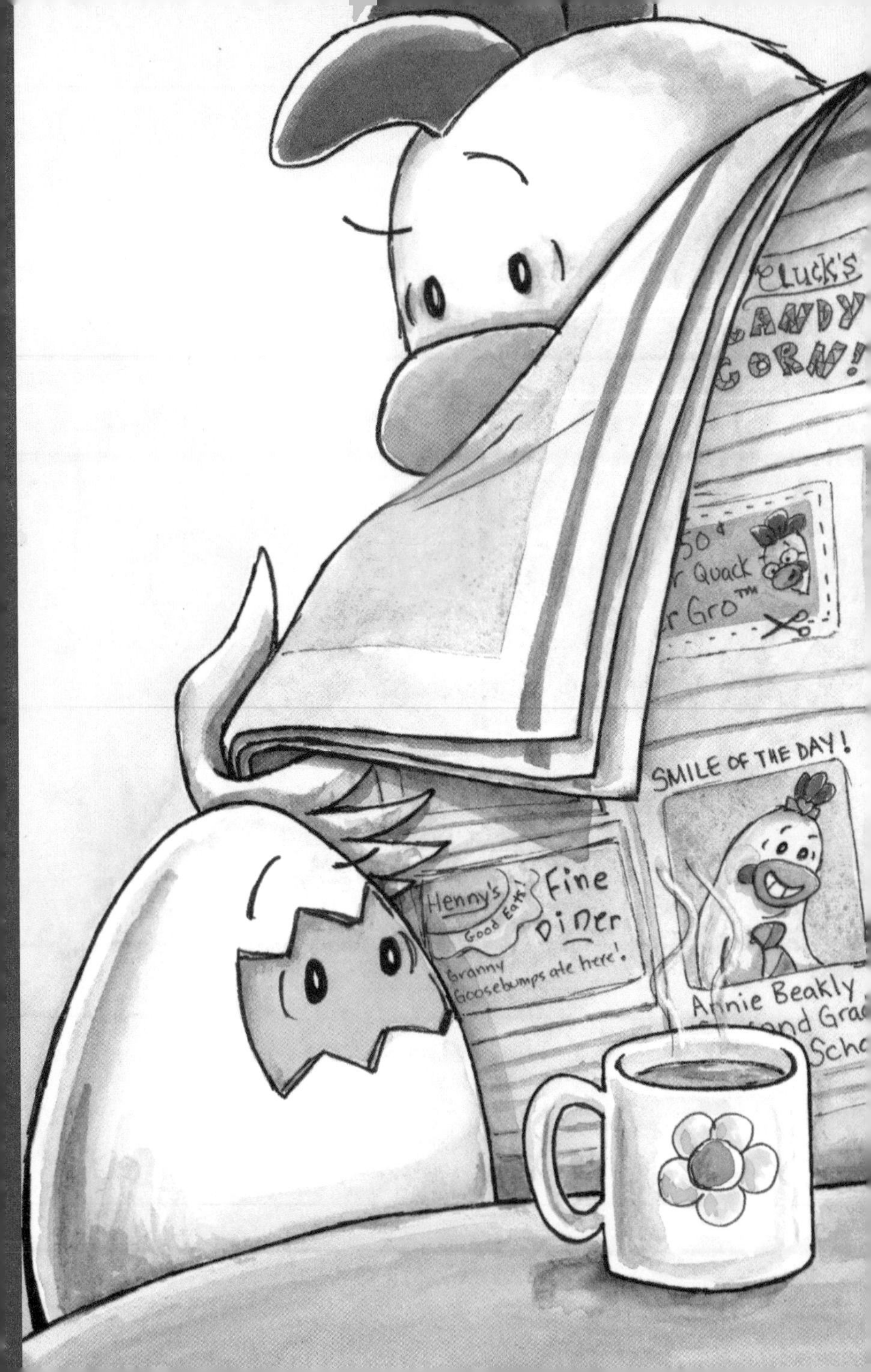

Cluck's
CANDY CORN!
50¢
r Quack
r Gro™
SMILE OF THE DAY!
Annie Beakly
Henny's
Good Eats!
Fine
DiNer
Granny
Goosebumps ate here!

THE FOWL TIMES

FAMOUS SINGER CHICKNAPPED!

by Sam Snood

Honey Comb was hooked from the Fowladelphia Opera House last night by new bad guy, Dr. Screech. Opera-goers saw Kung Pow Chicken with Dr. Screech. Where is Honey Comb now? Did Kung Pow Chicken <u>help</u> Dr. Screech snatch the singer?

Only bad guys wear masks! The reward for telling on Kung Pow Chicken has doubled. Just tell me.

$$ REWARD $$

Gordon almost choked on his cornflakes after reading what Sam Snood had written about him.

Mrs. Blue handed Gordon a glass of water.
He took a sip. Then Benny asked if they could go
back to Uncle Quack's lab for the day.

Yes.

YAY!

But listen to your
Uncle Quack.

Yes, Mom.

Unless he sounds a little
<u>cuckoo</u> today.

Mom!

We like when
he's <u>cuckoo</u>.

Gordon and Benny headed straight for Uncle Quack's lab. They hoped he had been able to find out more about Dr. Screech. They had to find a way to rescue Honey Comb and save the city! But this bad guy was a tough egg to crack.

As Gordon and Benny passed chickens on the street, they heard mad mumbles.

We want a hero, not a super zero!

Kung Pow Chicken chicknapped Honey Comb?!

Kung Pow Chicken looks like a super doofus in this photo!

Gordon was upset by what the chickens were saying. But Benny reminded him that a true hero helps out—no matter what other chickens say about him.

When Gordon and Benny got to the lab,
Uncle Quack had a lot to tell them.

Dr. Screech was testing a new invention at Mad Scientist School. It was called the Cone of Silence.

But Dr. Screech stayed inside the quiet cone WAY too long! It scrambled his brain!

Now he gets upset when things are too quiet.

That explains everything!

And Mom thought <u>Uncle Quack</u> was cuckoo.

I'm sure Dr. Screech is planning to use Honey Comb's powerful voice to shake <u>something</u> in this city to bits.

We just have to figure out what.

Ham and eggs! We have to rescue Miss Comb and save the city!

Gordon and Benny quickly changed into their super suits.

LET'S GET CRACKING!

HI-YAH!

Kung Pow Chicken and Egg Drop followed Uncle Quack up to the roof. Uncle Quack had made new <u>super</u> gadgets for his nephews. He gave them each a pair of Safe-T-Muffs™.

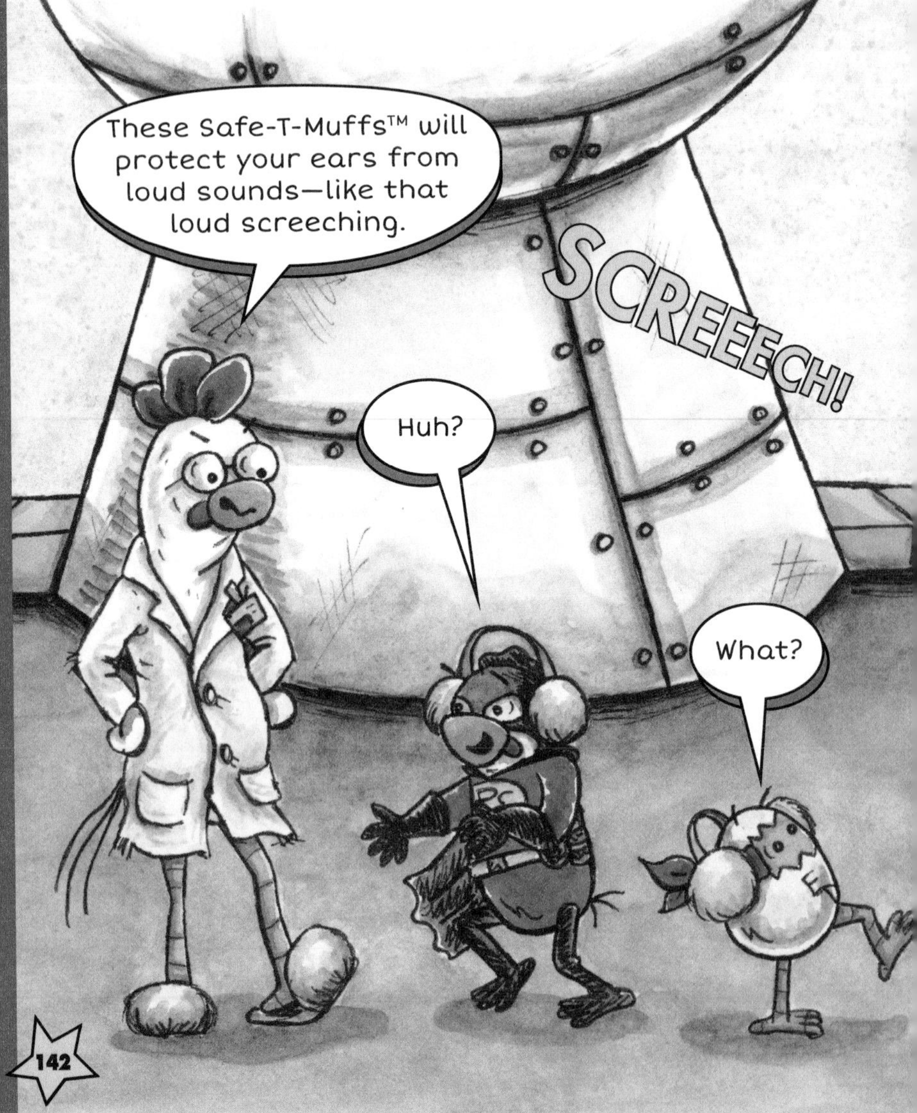

These Safe-T-Muffs™ will protect your ears from loud sounds—like that loud screeching.
SCREEEECH!
Huh?
What?

Then he gave his nephews a hang glider.

Now the superheroes were ready to fight the bad guy.

Dr. Screech's voice boomed through the air.
The city thundered with noise. Windows rattled!
Chickens bokked! Car alarms beeped!

Kung Pow Chicken took a deep breath. He
gritted his beak. Dr. Screech didn't scare <u>him</u>.

Kung Pow Chicken landed the Chicken-Wing™
next to Dr. Screech's hideout. It was a noisy
building. The heroes slipped in the front door
and put on their Safe-T-Muffs™. Kung Pow
Chicken flashed his Drumsticks of Doom.

They tiptoed from room to room, and floor to floor, and finally to the roof.

Kung Pow Chicken spotted Honey Comb. He rushed right over to her. Honey Comb tried to warn him.

But it was no use. Kung Pow Chicken couldn't hear a thing while wearing his Safe-T-Muffs™. A big claw snapped shut around him!

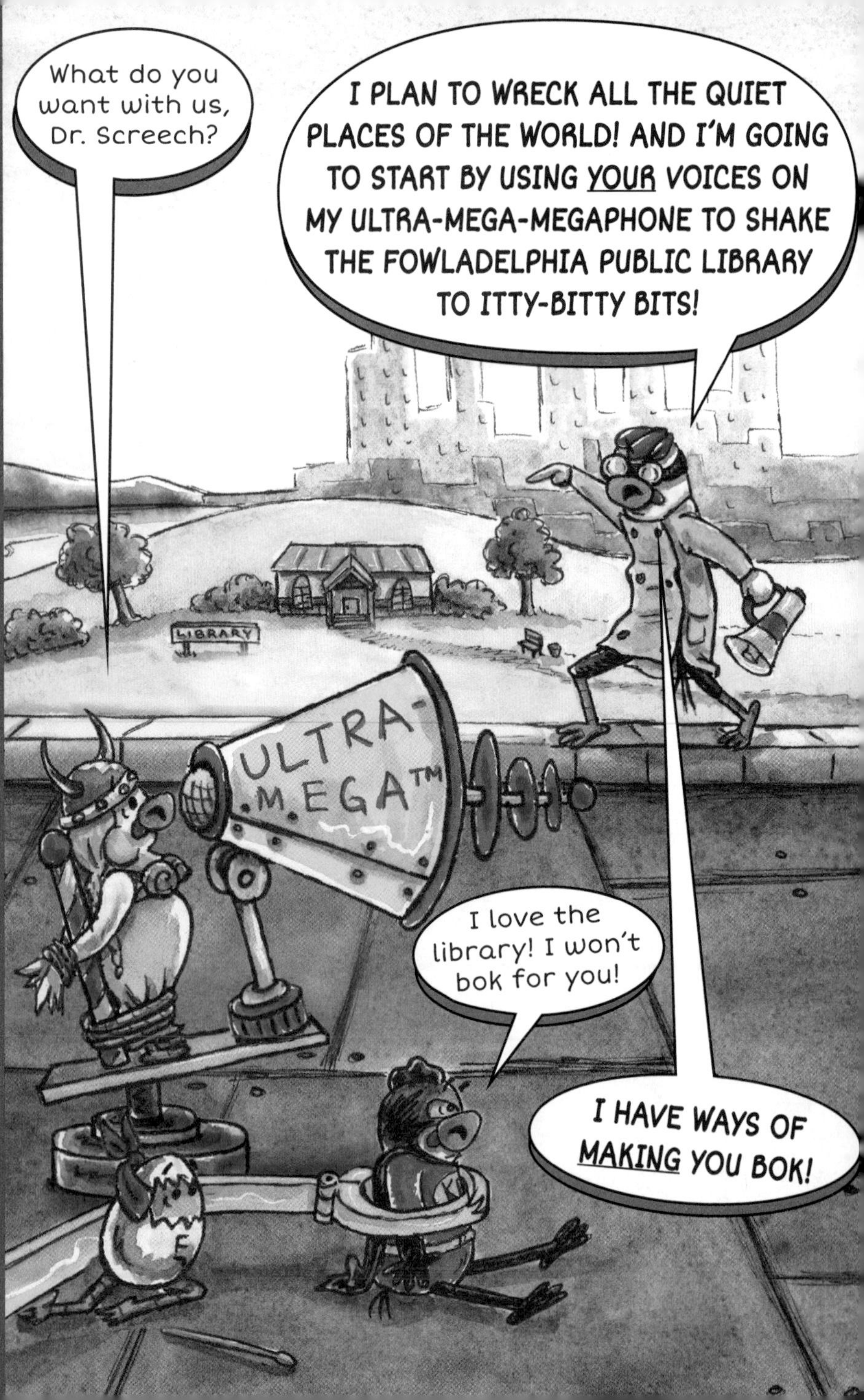
What do you want with us, Dr. Screech?
I PLAN TO WRECK ALL THE QUIET PLACES OF THE WORLD! AND I'M GOING TO START BY USING YOUR VOICES ON MY ULTRA-MEGA-MEGAPHONE TO SHAKE THE FOWLADELPHIA PUBLIC LIBRARY TO ITTY-BITTY BITS!
LIBRARY
ULTRA-MEGA™
I love the library! I won't bok for you!
I HAVE WAYS OF MAKING YOU BOK!

Just then, Egg Drop jumped out. He tossed a Drumstick of Doom to Kung Pow Chicken.

The hero caught it in his beak and smashed the claw! He was free!

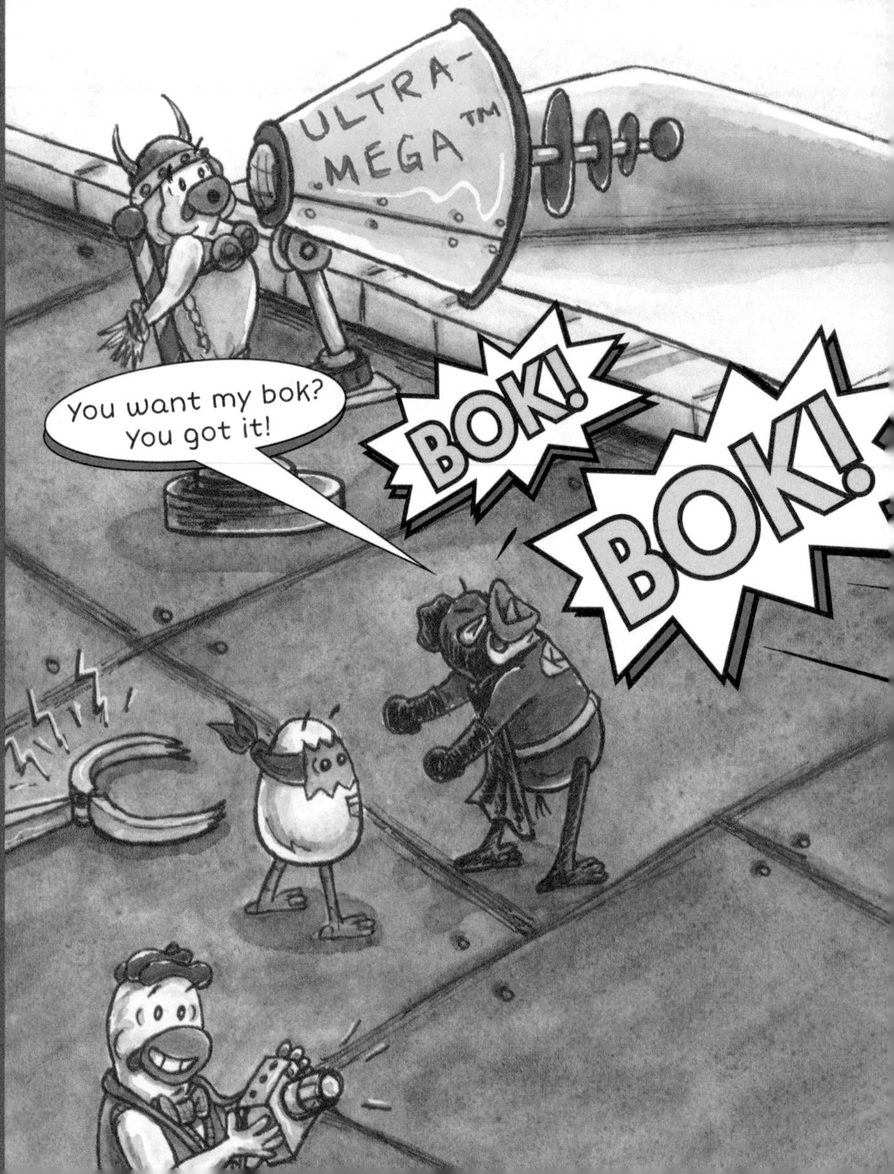
ULTRA-MEGA™
You want my bok? You got it!
BOK!
BOK!

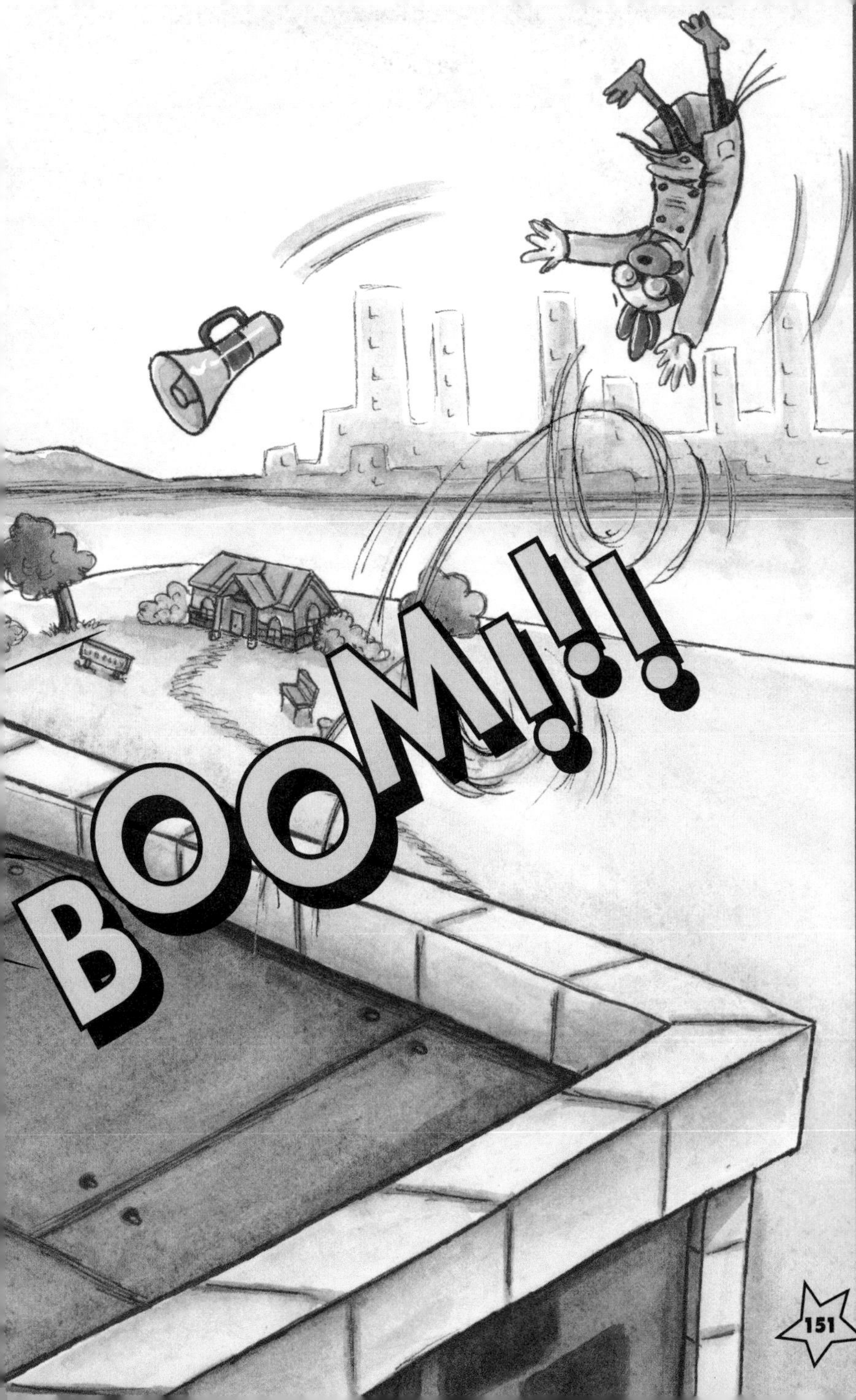
BOOM!!!

Dr. Screech flung his arms and legs out wide. He opened his flight suit to escape. But Kung Pow Chicken was ready with his Beak-A-Rang. He plucked Dr. Screech right out of the sky!

BEAK-A-RANG!

The next morning, Mrs. Blue was on the phone with Uncle Quack. She squawked excitedly and then hung up.

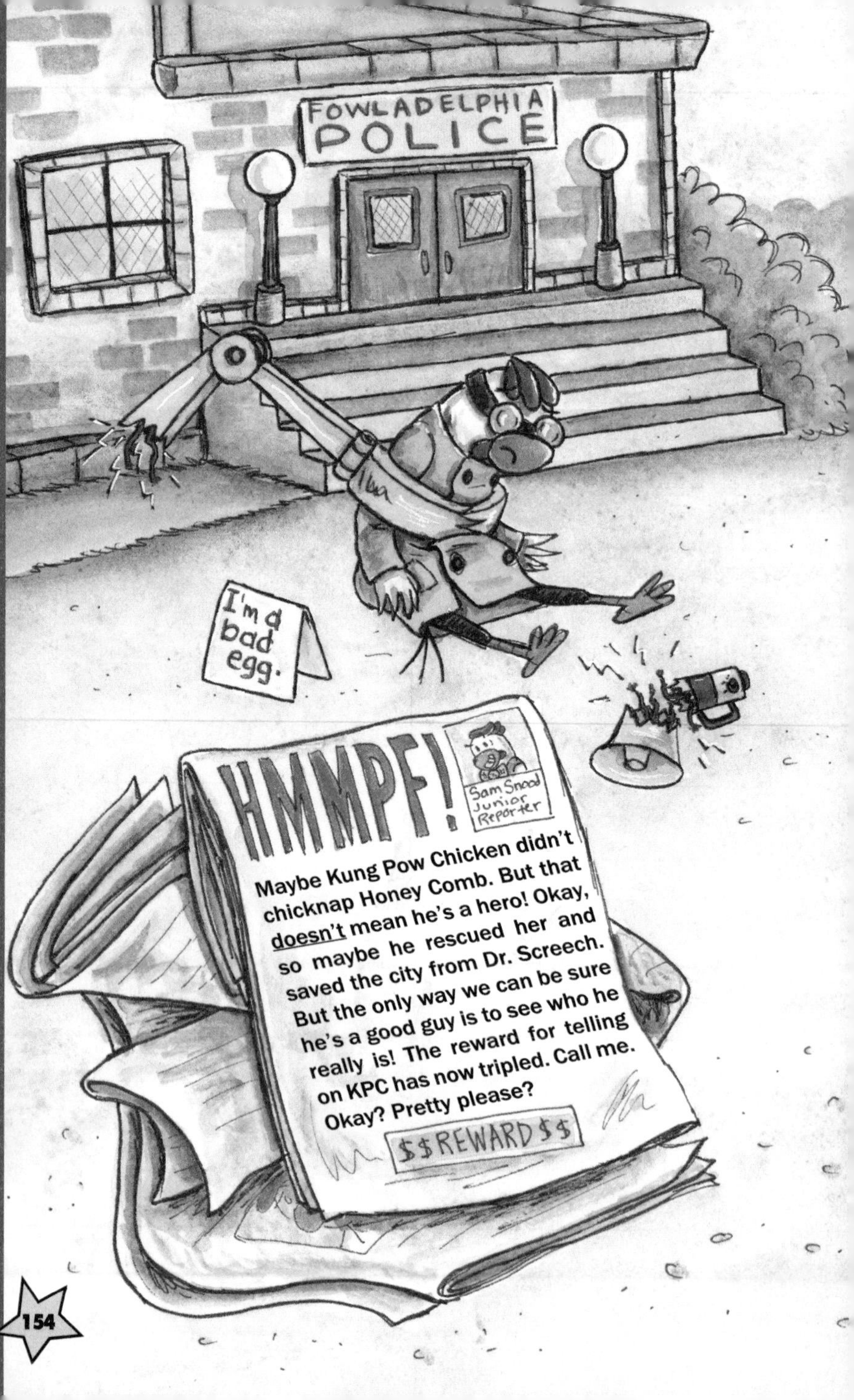
FOWLADELPHIA POLICE
I'm a bad egg.
HMMPF!
Sam Snood Junior Reporter
Maybe Kung Pow Chicken didn't chicknap Honey Comb. But that doesn't mean he's a hero! Okay, so maybe he rescued her and saved the city from Dr. Screech. But the only way we can be sure he's a good guy is to see who he really is! The reward for telling on KPC has now tripled. Call me. Okay? Pretty please?
$$REWARD$$

KUNG POW CHICKEN ★

PROVE YOUR SUPERHERO KNOW-HOW!

What are some of Gordon's superpowers? Name three!

A compound word is made up of two words that come together to make one new word. Break these compound words into two words to figure out their meanings: *superpower, newspaper,* and *rooftops.*

Benny tells Gordon that, "a true hero helps out—no matter what other chickens say about him." Is this good advice? Why or why not?

What is Dr. Screech's evil plan?

Sam Snood does not believe Kung Pow Chicken is a hero. Pretend you are a reporter who believes he <u>is</u> a hero. Write an article about how he saved Honey Comb.

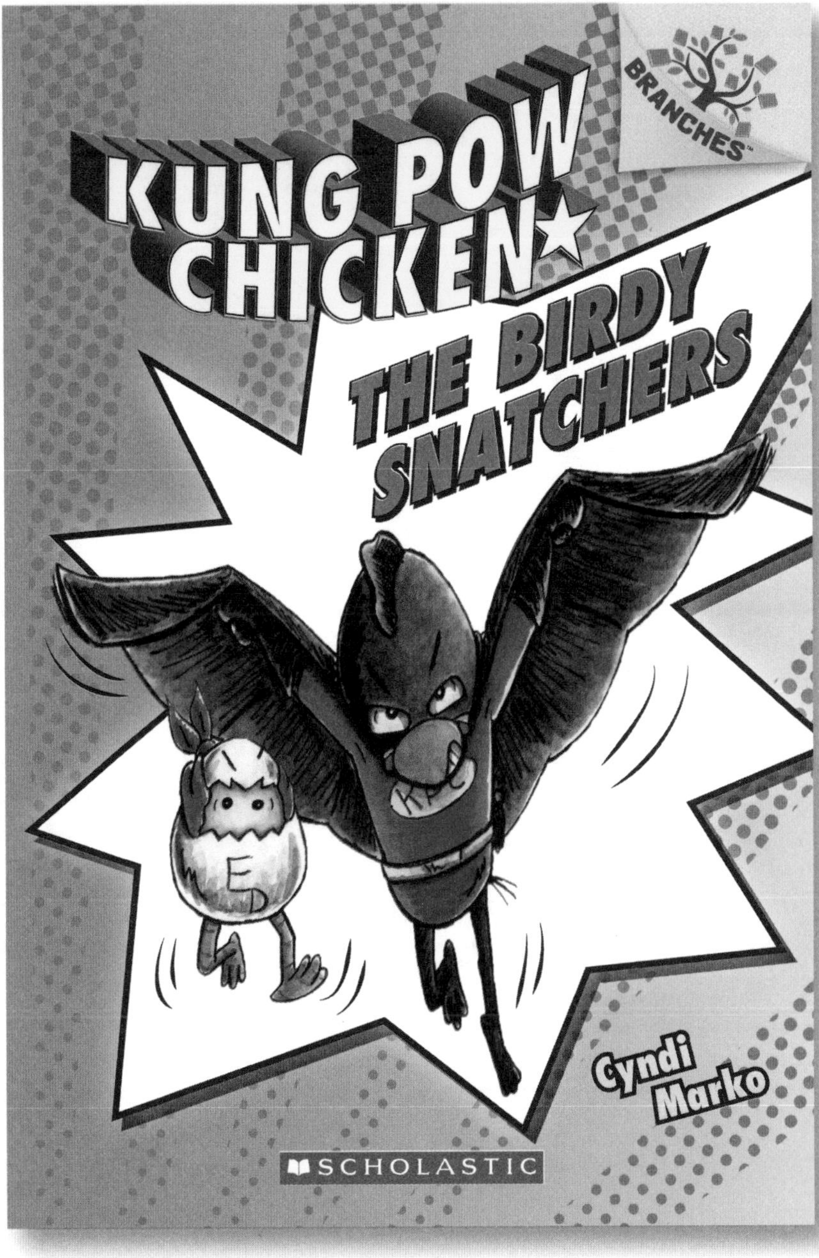
KUNG POW CHICKEN
THE BIRDY SNATCHERS
BRANCHES
Cyndi Marko
SCHOLASTIC

SEE-THRU-U TM
QUACK LABS

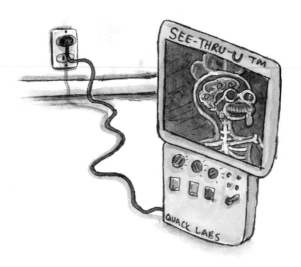

TABLE OF CONTENTS

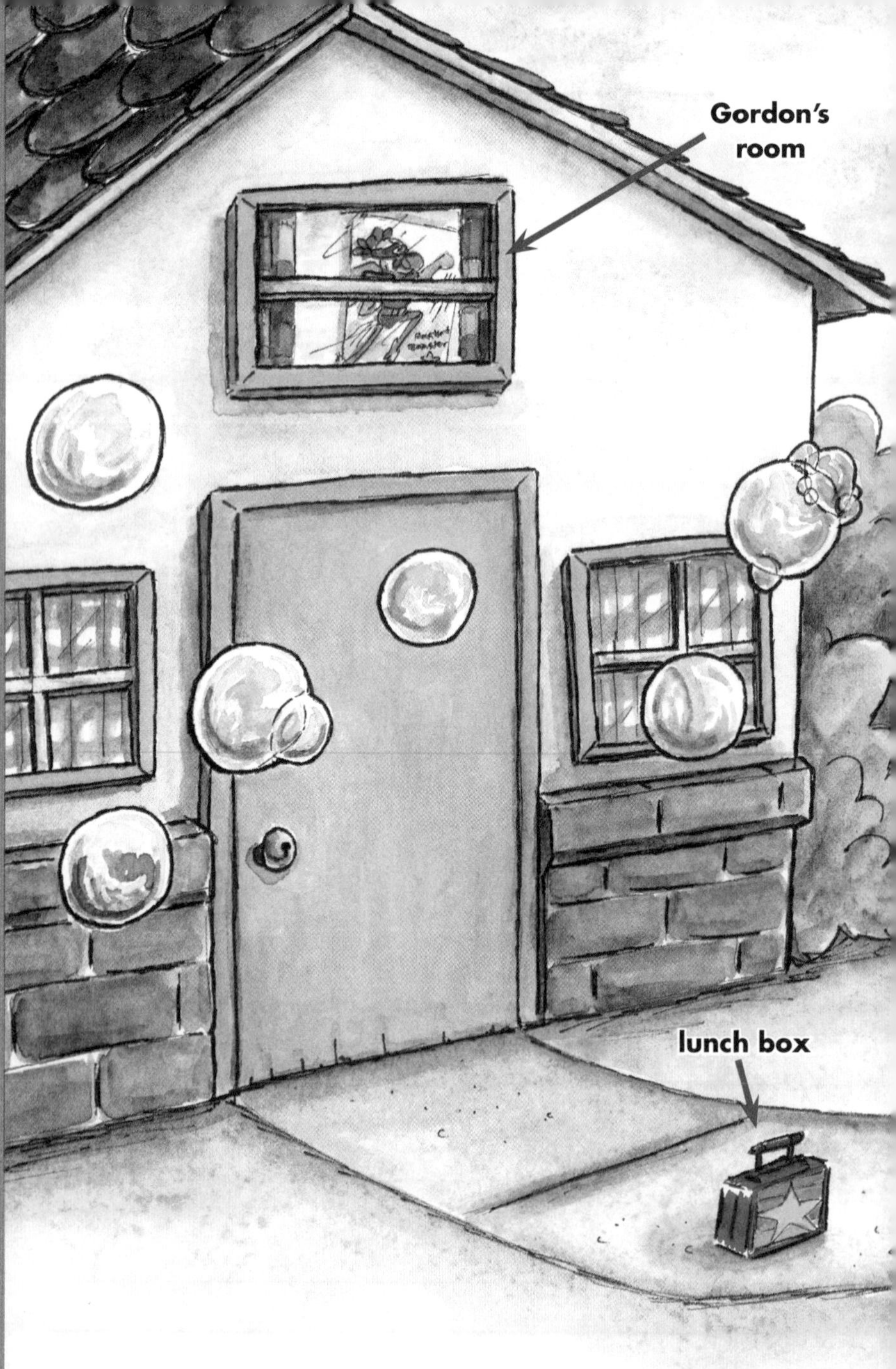

Gordon's room
lunch box

glasses

comb

wattle

school tie

tail feathers

Gordon Blue seemed like an ordinary chicken.

He lived with his ordinary family in the city of Fowladelphia.

It was an ordinary city. (Except for all the bad guys.)

And Gordon went to an ordinary school with other ordinary chickens.

But Gordon had a <u>super</u> secret.

When Gordon was younger, he fell into a vat of toxic sludge! Uncle Quack rescued him.

But the toxic sludge had given Gordon superpowers.

If bad guys are up to no good, Gordon's tail feathers tingle.

Then he slips into his super suit to fight bad guys as:

KUNG POW CHICKEN!

With his sidekick, Egg Drop!

Being a superhero wasn't easy.

Gordon liked having superpowers. But he wanted to meet other superheroes he could ask about super stuff.

Gordon liked catching bad guys. But it was tricky chasing them when his mom was around.

Kung Pow Chicken had already battled two bad guys. He had saved the city twice! Now Fowladelphia was quiet and safe.

167

With no bad guys to fight, Kung Pow Chicken was old news.

Snoopy reporter Sam Snood had found another chicken for the front page.

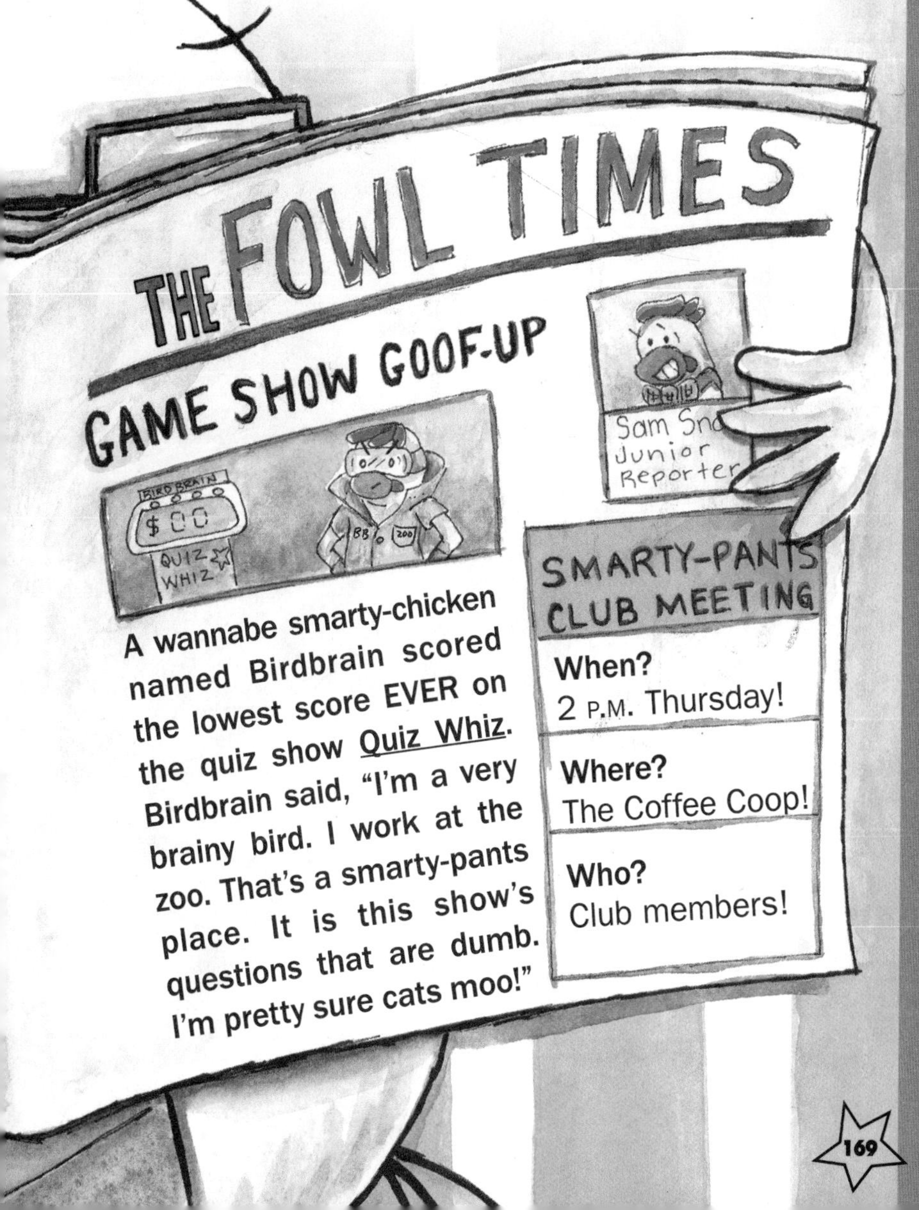
THE FOWL TIMES
GAME SHOW GOOF-UP
BIRD BRAIN
$00
QUIZ WHIZ
BB
ZOO
A wannabe smarty-chicken named Birdbrain scored the lowest score EVER on the quiz show Quiz Whiz. Birdbrain said, “I’m a very brainy bird. I work at the zoo. That’s a smarty-pants place. It is this show’s questions that are dumb. I’m pretty sure cats moo!”
Sam Sno
Junior Reporter
SMARTY-PANTS CLUB MEETING
When?
2 P.M. Thursday!
Where?
The Coffee Coop!
Who?
Club members!

There were no bad guys to catch. So Gordon was <u>super</u> bored. He was starting to wonder if he would be bored for the rest of his life.

Gordon got ready for another ordinary day at
school.

Mrs. Blue squeezed Gordon and Benny tight.

The walk to school was a bit strange.

Gordon dropped Benny off at kindergarten.

Then he walked to his second grade classroom. He sat next to his friend Annie.

Gordon's teacher, Mr. Giblets, was writing on the board.

The classroom speaker crackled. Gordon and his classmates grew quiet. They waited for their principal to give the morning news.

Good morning, Sunnyside School! All students are to leave right now. GO HOME! Teachers, come to the food-eating room. NOW! That is all. Have a nice day.

Gordon, that wasn't the principal's voice!

TINGLE!

Gordon's birdy senses started to tingle. A bad guy was up to no good.

Mr. Giblets left the classroom. He didn't say good-bye to his students. He just kept bokking about brains.

Gordon peeked out the door. Mr. Giblets and the rest of the teachers were shuffling down the hallway to the lunchroom. They were ALL acting weird.

Gordon <u>had</u> to find his little brother! It was superhero time.

Gordon ran to Benny's classroom.

The brothers found a good place to hide.

Gordon opened his lunch box.

LET'S GET CRACKING!

Finally!

Kung Pow Chicken and Egg Drop tiptoed down
the hallway. They heard something weird.

Then they tiptoed inside.

They belly-crawled over to the lunch counter and hid behind a jumbo-size can of creamed corn. But they weren't alone.

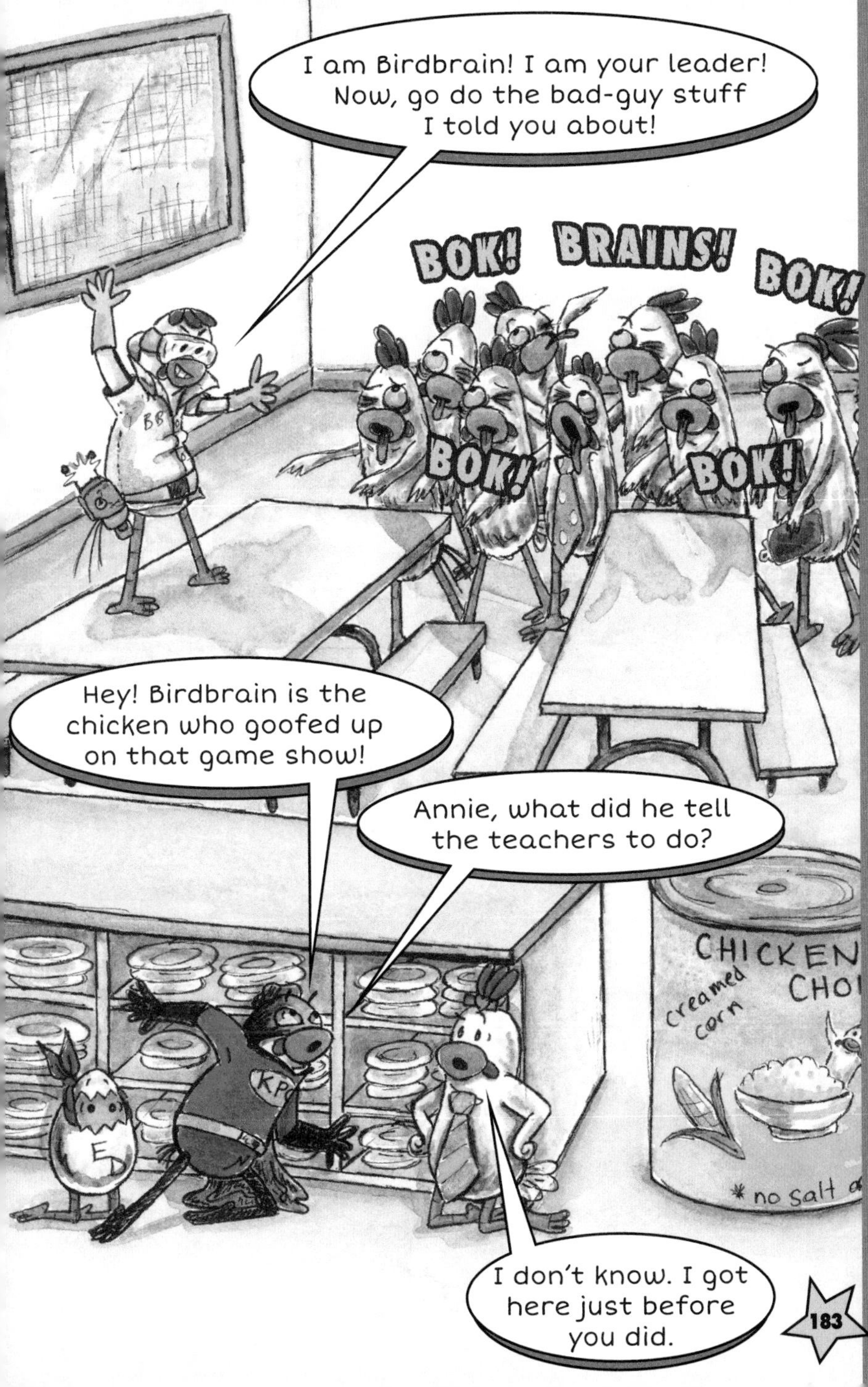
I am Birdbrain! I am your leader! Now, go do the bad-guy stuff I told you about!
BOK! BRAINS! BOK!
BOK! BOK!
Hey! Birdbrain is the chicken who goofed up on that game show!
Annie, what did he tell the teachers to do?
I don't know. I got here just before you did.
CHICKEN CHO
creamed corn
* no salt

Kung Pow Chicken didn't know Birdbrain's plan. But he knew Birdbrain <u>had</u> to be stopped. He told Annie to stay put. Then he flashed his Drumsticks of Doom. It was time to get cracking.

Kung Pow Chicken and Egg Drop jumped out from behind the creamed corn.

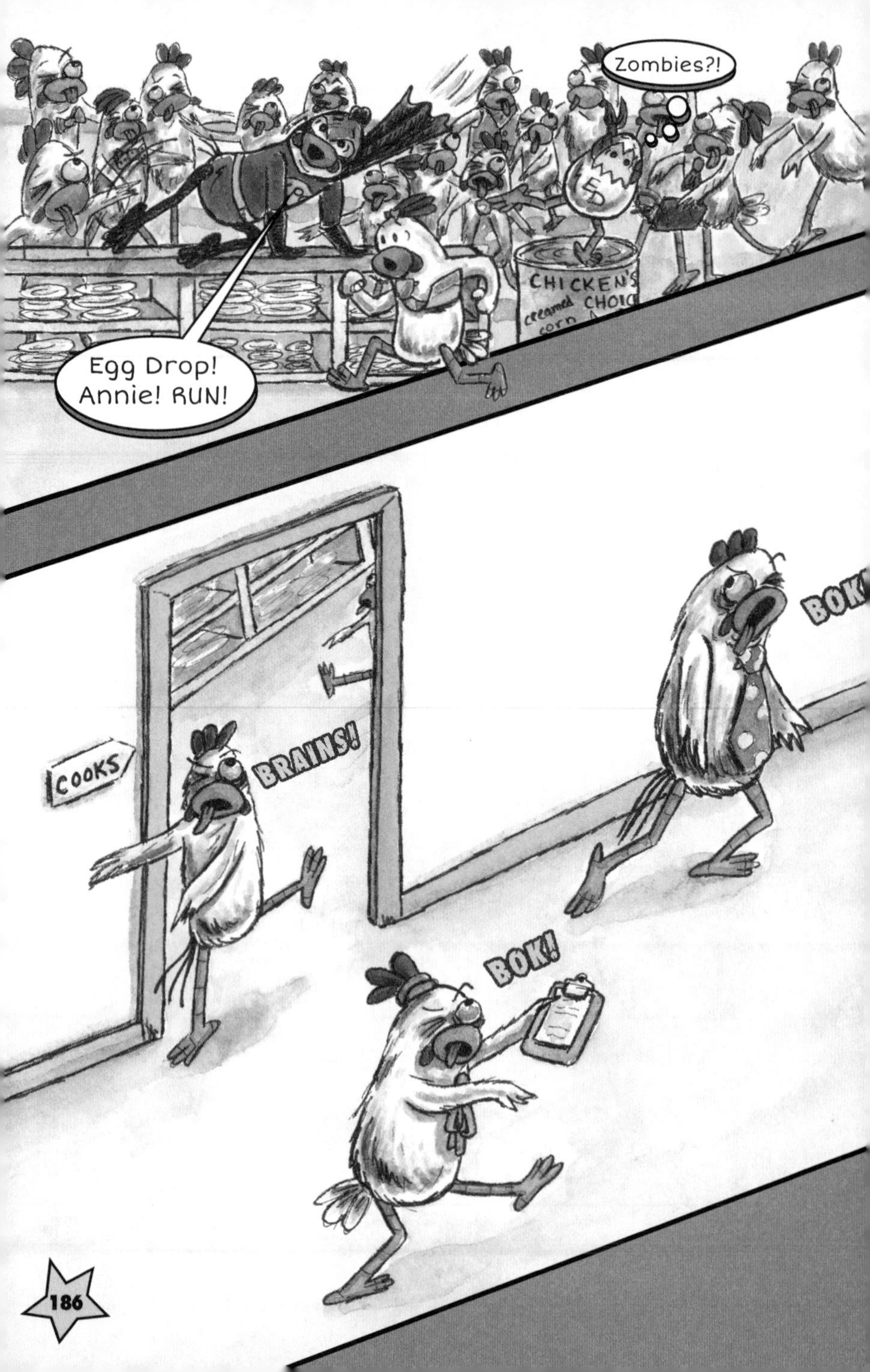
Zombies?!
CHICKEN'S creamed corn CHOICE
Egg Drop!
Annie! RUN!
COOKS
BRAINS!
BOK!
BOK!

Kung Pow Chicken, Egg Drop, and Annie burst out of the kitchen. They ran down the hallway. The zombies were right on their tail feathers!

The superheroes and Annie ran outside. Kung Pow Chicken held the doors shut. Egg Drop pushed a hockey stick through the handles. The zombies would have to find another way out.

Well, that was weird!

Yeah! What kind of bad guy doesn't want to battle?

The kind who has an army of zombies?

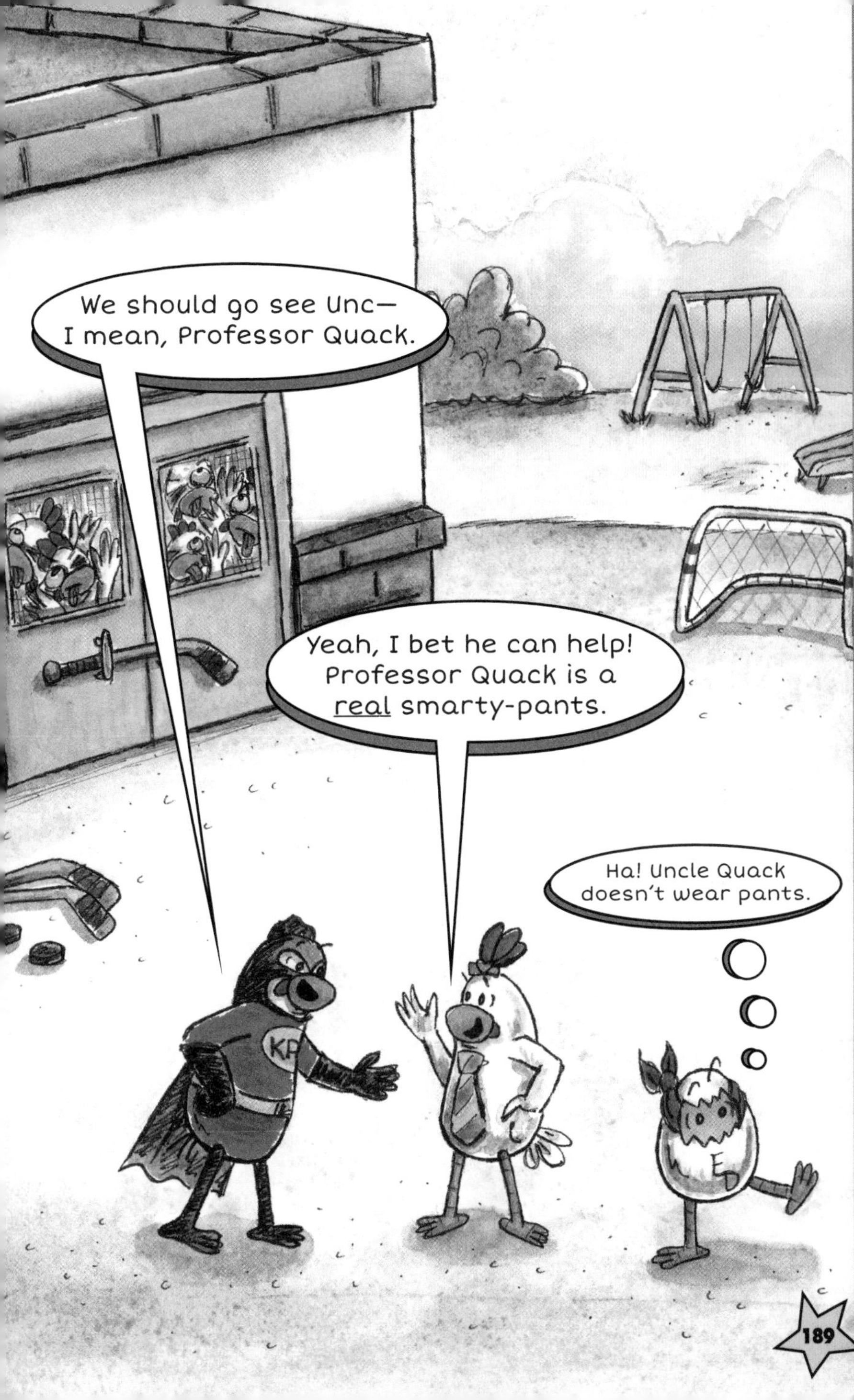
We should go see Unc—
I mean, Professor Quack.
Yeah, I bet he can help!
Professor Quack is a
real smarty-pants.
Ha! Uncle Quack
doesn't wear pants.

Kung Pow Chicken took out his Beak-Phone.
He hit the AUTO-BEAK button. The Beak-Mobile
showed up right away.

Wow! Cool bike!
Can I come with
you guys?

Head home,
Annie. You'll be
safer there.

No fair!
I can help!

Just call if
you need us.

Fine. But
you're not the
boss of me.

I like _her_.
She's spunky!

Kung Pow Chicken and Egg Drop rode to Uncle Quack's lab. Their uncle was waiting for them.

Uncle Quack held up a copy of the <u>Fowl Times</u>.

Uncle Quack, what do you know about Birdbrain?

I don't know this Birdbrain guy. But I watch scary movies. So I know all about zombies. Zombies want brains.

The zombie teachers were all saying <u>brains</u>!

But why would a bad guy want brains?!

SMARTY-PANTS MEETING TODAY!

KPC

They didn't know what Birdbrain was up to. But they did all agree that zombies were bad. The heroes needed to find out more about Birdbrain and about zombies.

We need to find Birdbrain!

But what if WE get snatched?

I have a new gadget that should keep you safe.

SMARTY-PANTS MEETING TODAY!

Uncle Quack grabbed two shiny helmets.

He put them on his nephews' heads.

Kung Pow Chicken and Egg Drop's brains were safe from zombies. They were ready to catch the bad guy! They just had to find his hideout.

The heroes said good-bye to Uncle Quack.

Bring back a zombie for my See-Thru-U™ machine! I'd love to see inside his head!

Okay. And see what you can find out about Birdbrain while we go after him.

To the Beak-Mobile!

Birdy Snatched!

The superheroes rode up and down the city
streets. Brain-hungry zombies were everywhere!
They were at the Public Library, the Chess Club,
and even the smarty-college, Fowl Tech.

RIIING!

Kung Pow Chicken answered his Beak-Phone.
It was Annie Beakly.

Hey. I did a Gaggle search and found clues. Not only did Birdbrain get EVERY question wrong on that game show, but he was booed off the stage! AND he <u>tried</u> to join the Smarty-Pants Club. But after that show, they wouldn't let him in.

Thanks, Annie!

Kung Pow Chicken told Annie to stay safe. He put away his Beak-Phone.

The heroes kept driving. Soon they spotted
a noisy pack of zombies by Uncle Quack's lab.
The brain-hungry zombies had snatched Uncle
Quack!

Kung Pow Chicken zoomed the Beak-Mobile
through the zombie mob. Zombies scrambled
out of the way.

Egg Drop snatched his uncle away from the zombies. But it was too late: Uncle Quack was a zombie.

BOK!

BOK!

BOK!

BRAAINS!

BRAAINS!

BRAAINS!

To the See-Thru-U™ machine! We have to see if his brain is still there!

Uncle Quack must have run out of tinfoil! Good thing we're wearing *our* Zom-B-Gones™!

Kung Pow Chicken and Egg Drop zoomed
to the lab. They sat their uncle down behind the
See-Thru-U™ machine. Egg Drop turned it on.

Phew! His brain
is still there!

His BRAIN! Wait a minute!
That's it! Uncle Quack is the biggest
brain in town! Birdbrain's zombies aren't
snatching BRAINS, they're snatching
<u>BRAINY</u> chickens!

DANGER

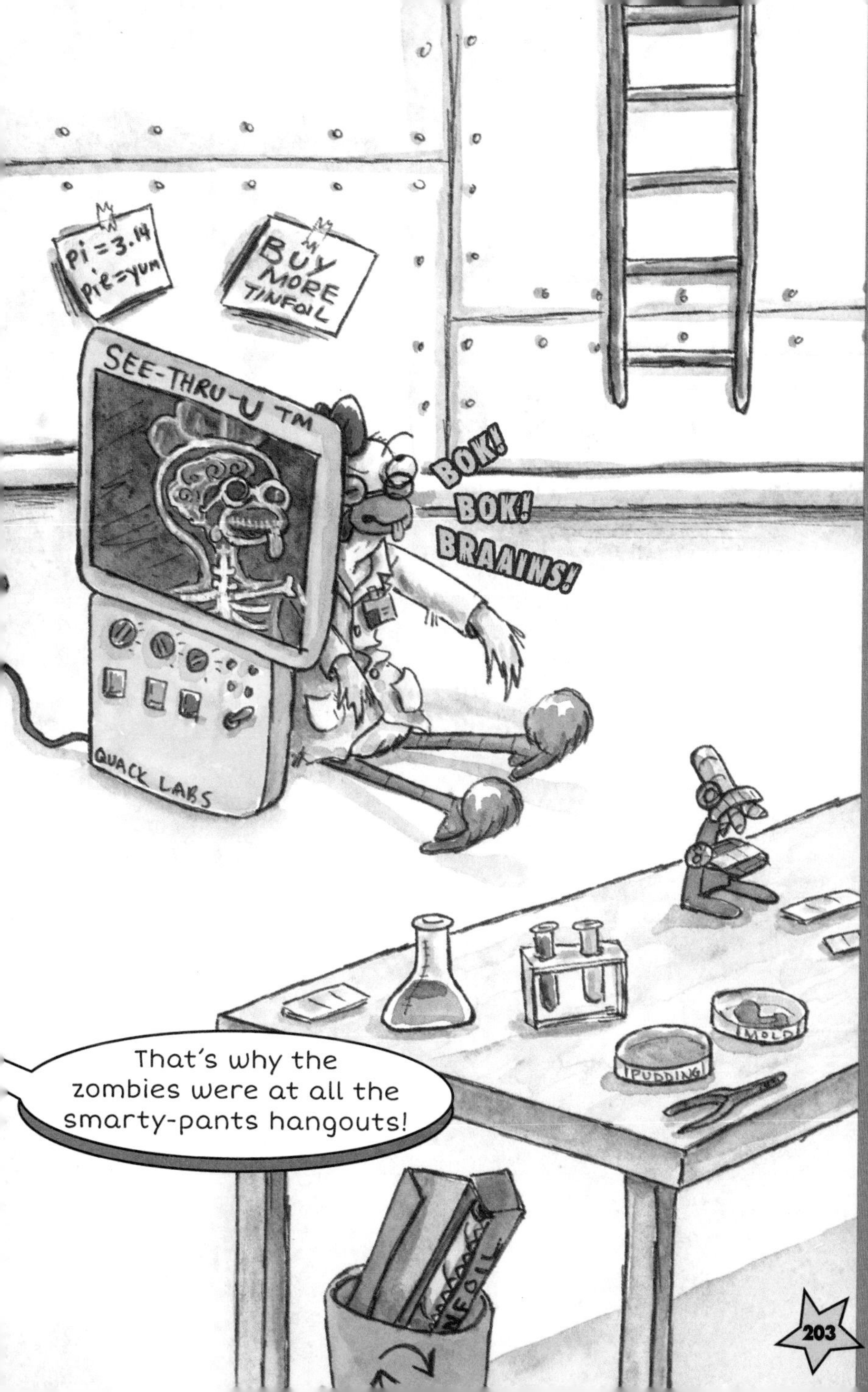
pi = 3.14
pie = yum
BUY MORE TINFOIL
SEE-THRU-U TM
QUACK LABS
BOK!
BOK!
BRAAINS!
PUDDING
MOLD
That's why the zombies were at all the smarty-pants hangouts!

But WHY is Birdbrain turning smart chickens into zombies?

I don't know, but the zombies aren't <u>bad</u> guys. They're just smart chickens acting like dummies.

We <u>need</u> to find Birdbrain.

Let's follow some zombies! They should lead us to Birdbrain's hideout.

Okay, but we can't leave Uncle Quack alone. I'll ask Annie to zombie-sit.

Kung Pow Chicken called Annie. She showed up right away. Then the heroes went looking for zombies.

Kung Pow Chicken and Egg Drop spotted a pack of zombies. They parked the Beak-Mobile and followed the zombies around the corner.

The heroes came beak-to-beak with a huge zombie army!

But the zombies couldn't sniff the heroes' brains through their helmets. So Egg Drop snatched the Zom-B-Gone™ from Kung Pow Chicken's head. He took his own off, too.

Ack! What are you doing?!

Trust me!

The zombies smelled brains.

BOK! BOK! BRAINS!

Kung Pow Chicken tried to escape. But the
zombies lifted him up into the air. They grabbed
Egg Drop, too.

The heroes had been birdy snatched!

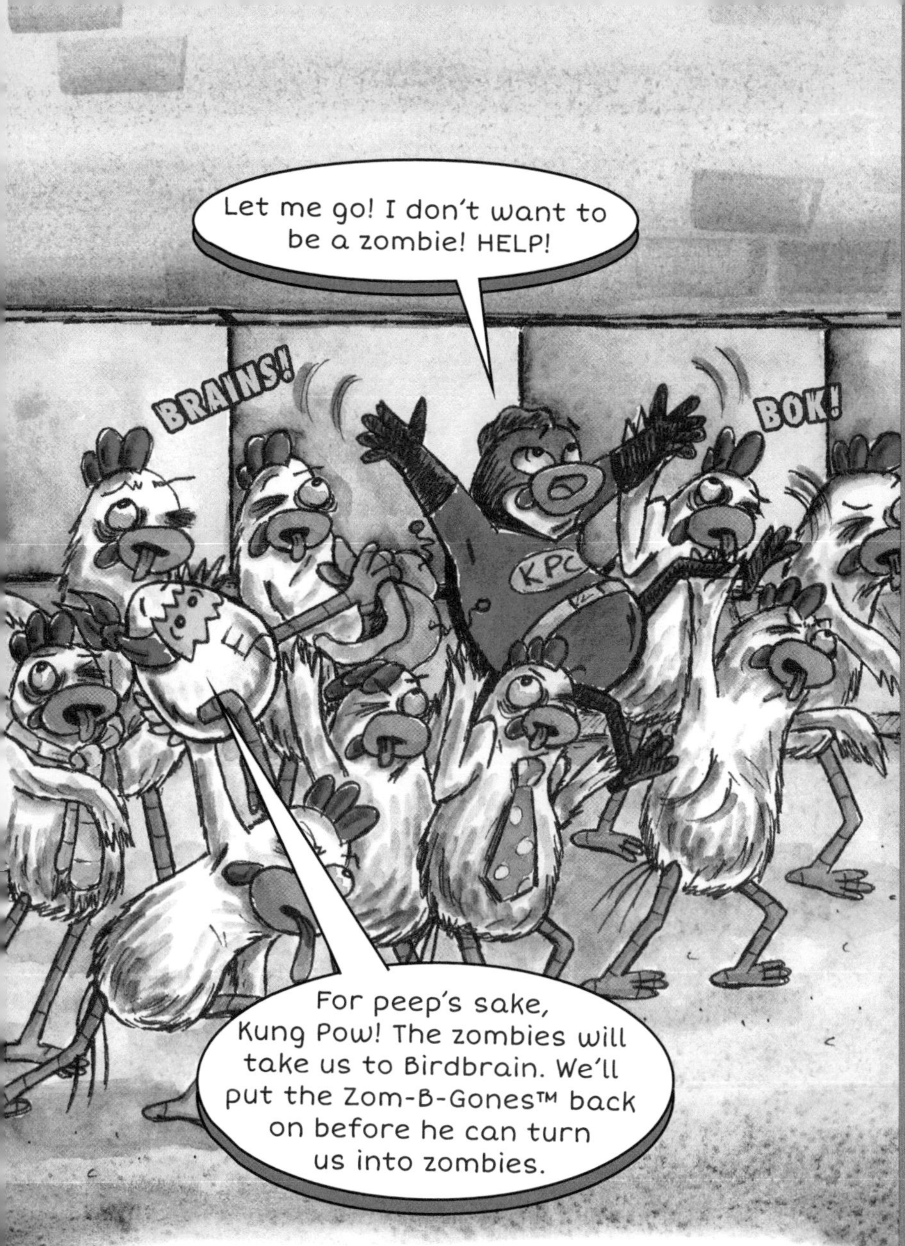
Let me go! I don't want to be a zombie! HELP!
BRAINS!
BOK!
KPC
For peep's sake, Kung Pow! The zombies will take us to Birdbrain. We'll put the Zom-B-Gones™ back on before he can turn us into zombies.

Kung Pow Chicken stopped struggling.

After a long march, the zombies stopped at the Fowladelphia Zoo. They dumped Kung Pow Chicken and Egg Drop in an empty pit. The heroes were trapped!

Kung Pow Chicken and Egg Drop put their Zom-B-Gones™ back on. They huddled on an iceberg.

Of course the zoo is Birdbrain's hideout. He works here!

We got snatched for nothing.

But zombie surfing was worth it!

BRRR!

BRRR!

Just then, Birdbrain poked his beak through the bars.

Well, well. Look what the zombies dragged in!

POLAR BEAR PIT

CLOSED FOR CLEANING

Birdbrain! Turn the smarty-chickens back to normal!

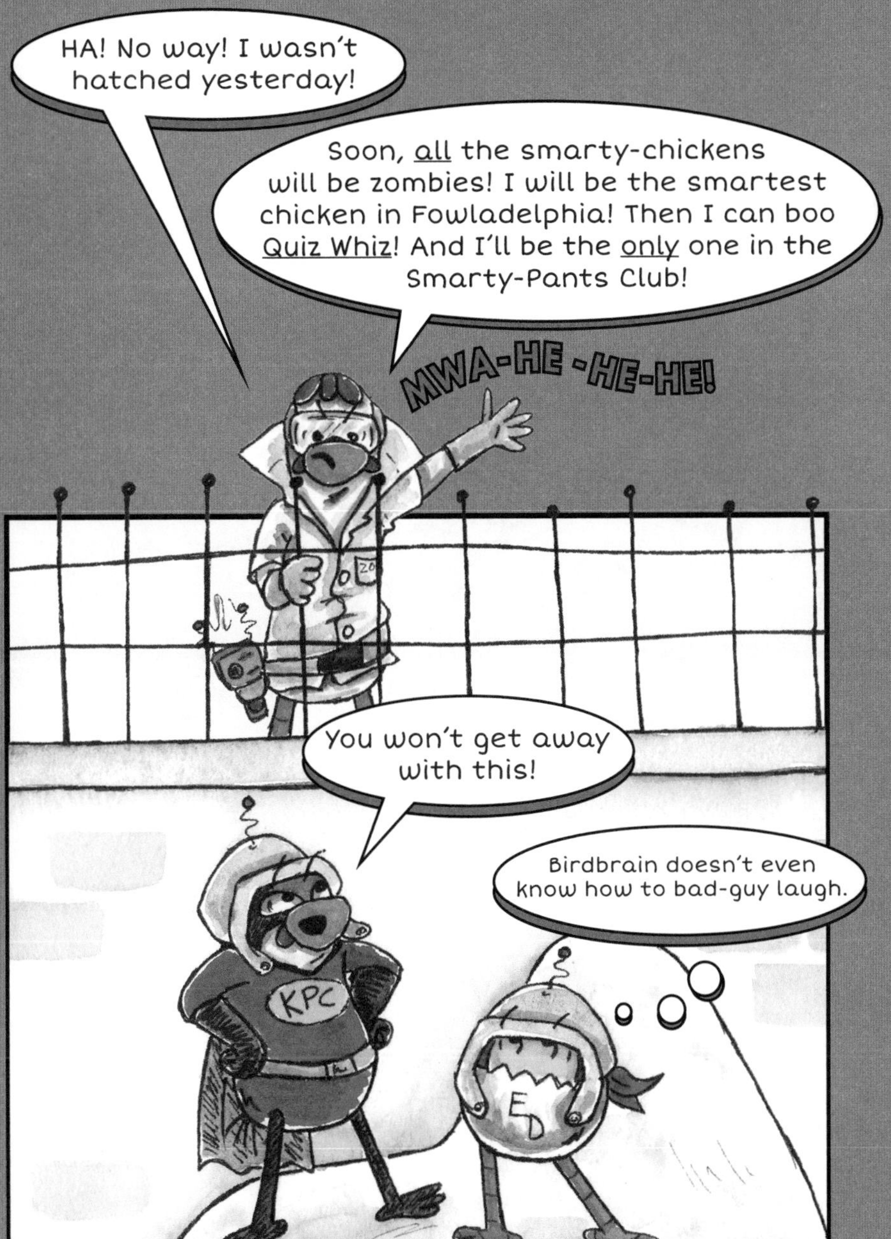
HA! No way! I wasn't hatched yesterday!
Soon, all the smarty-chickens will be zombies! I will be the smartest chicken in Fowladelphia! Then I can boo Quiz Whiz! And I'll be the only one in the Smarty-Pants Club!
MWA-HE -HE-HE!
You won't get away with this!
Birdbrain doesn't even know how to bad-guy laugh.

Birdbrain held up a strange-looking gadget.

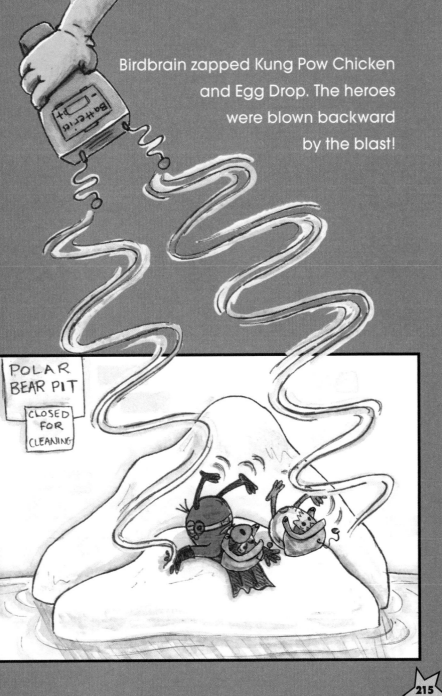

Birdbrain zapped Kung Pow Chicken and Egg Drop. The heroes were blown backward by the blast!

POLAR BEAR PIT

CLOSED FOR CLEANING

But Uncle Quack's Zom-B-Gones™ had kept their brains safe.

Birdbrain fell for their zombie act. Then he and his zombies left the zoo.

Kung Pow Chicken and Egg Drop were stuck on the iceberg. But at least they weren't zombies. They took off their helmets.

POLAR
BEAR PIT
CLOSED
FOR
CLEANING

Suddenly, the Chicken-Wing™ swooped down from the sky. It passed over Kung Pow Chicken and Egg Drop.

Ham and eggs!

Who's flying our Chicken-Wing™?!

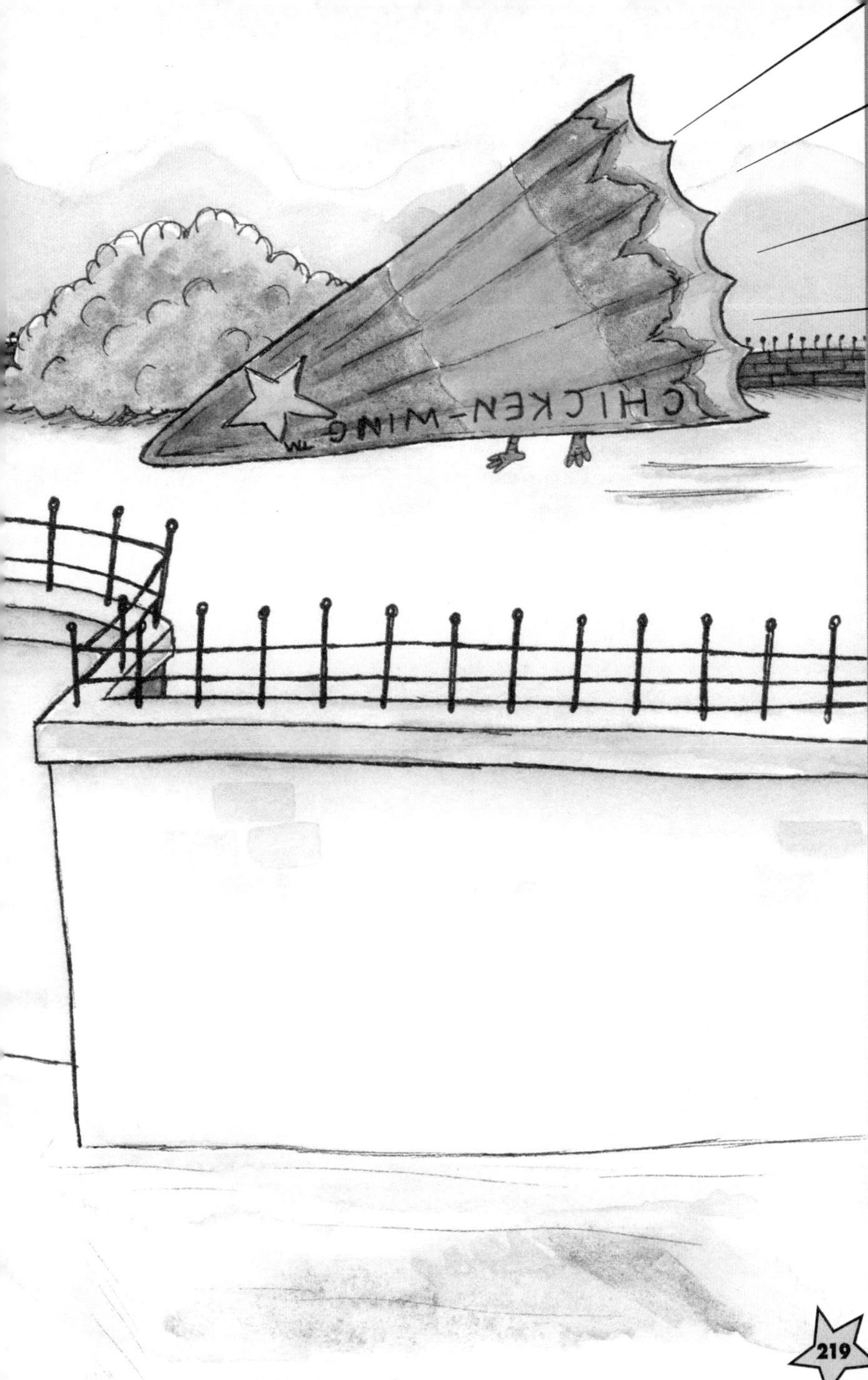
CHICKEN-WING
TM

The mystery flyer snagged the heroes and
lifted them up into the air!

The Chicken-Wing™ landed outside the zoo.

Kung Pow Chicken and Egg Drop turned to face their rescuer. A superhero stood before them. Or, it was a chicken <u>dressed</u> like a superhero.

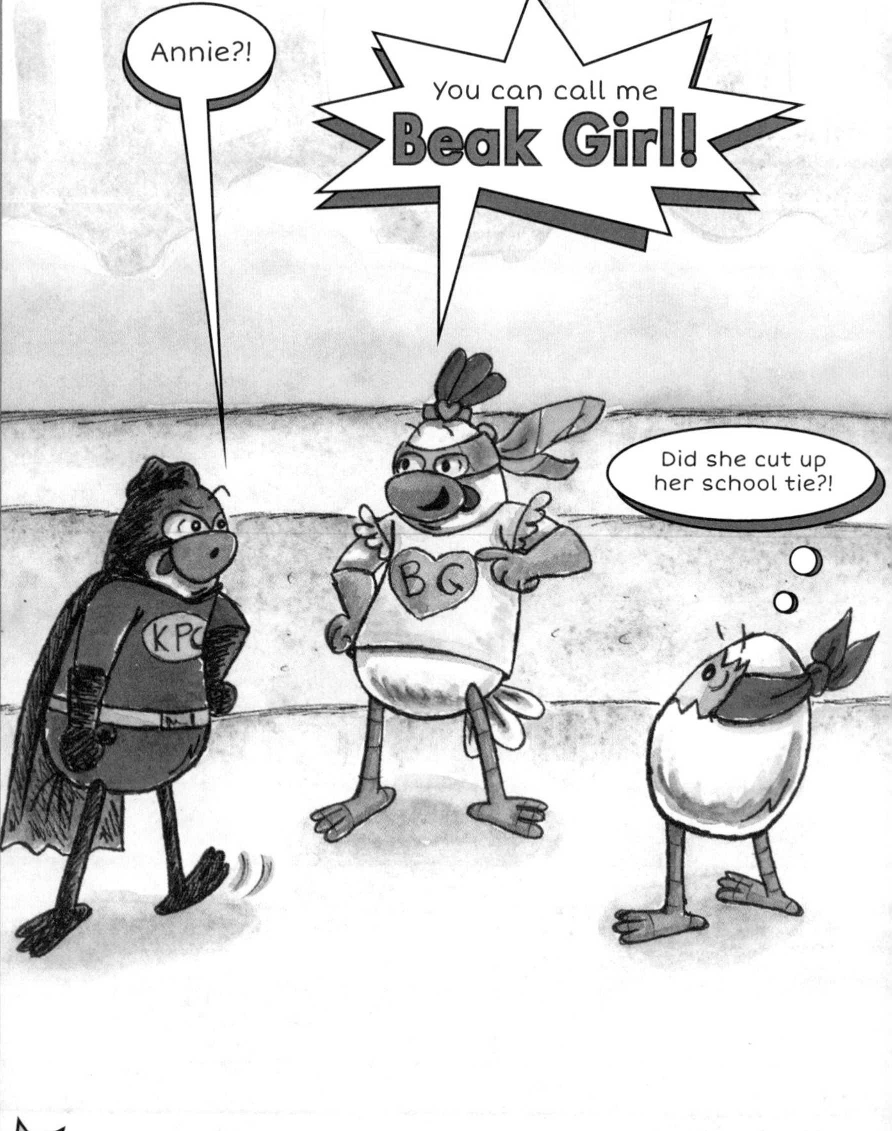
Annie?!
You can call me
Beak Girl!
Did she cut up
her school tie?!

Kung Pow Chicken was happy to be rescued. But he was <u>not</u> happy to see Annie. Now he was cranky.

What are <u>you</u> doing here?

I was zombie-sitting Professor Quack. Then you "pocket dialed" me from your Beak-Phone. When I heard Birdbrain zap you, I just had to help!

But you should be keeping Professor Quack safe!

Oh, he's fine. I put him in his empty pool with a beach ball.

Kung Pow is ALWAYS sitting on his phone!

There was a bad guy on the loose. Kung Pow Chicken didn't have time to bok at Beak Girl.

We need to find Birdbrain and get his Zombie-Zapper. Then we can zap the zombies back to normal.

Birdbrain said he was going to the Smarty-Pants Club meeting!

And the Fowl Times said the meeting is at the Coffee Coop!

To the Coffee Coop!

The three heroes burst into the Coffee Coop. But they were too late. Birdbrain had already zapped all the Smarty-Pants Club members with his Zombie-Zapper! The heroes were outnumbered.

Annie hid under a table. Kung Pow Chicken flung the Beak-A-Rang. It knocked the zapper out of Birdbrain's hands.

Egg Drop stopped. He dropped. And he
rolled like thunder.

The zombies swarmed Kung Pow Chicken and Egg Drop. The heroes didn't have their Zom-B-Gones™ to keep them safe. They tried to fight back. There were just too many zombies.

But Beak Girl couldn't bear to see her heroes in trouble. She grabbed the Zombie-Zapper.

Kung Pow Chicken quickly turned the dial to CHICKEN. He pressed the button and spun in a circle.

Kung Pow Chicken turned the dial again—
this time to ZOMBIE. He zapped Birdbrain with the
Zombie-Zapper.

Kung Pow Chicken, Egg Drop, and Beak Girl rushed to the lab to zap Uncle Quack. They told him everything.

Beak Girl took off her mask. She was just ordinary Annie Beakly again.

Thanks for your help, Annie. But you don't have superpowers to keep you safe. Next time, leave the bad-guy fighting to the _real_ superheroes.

Hmmph. Well, I _did_ save your tail feathers twice today!

Maybe she needs a sidekick?

After Annie left, the heroes put away their super suits. Another bad egg had been cracked—just in time for dinner.

I can't wait for dessert!

BOK! BOK! BRAINS!

TEN FOOT POLE

THE FOWL TIMES

SUPER BEAK GIRL!

Sam Snood Junior Reporter

by Sam Snood

A new superhero named Beak Girl saved Fowladelphia from the Birdy Snatchers. Birdbrain, the game show goof-up, was behind all the zombies. There was a battle at the Coffee Coop. And the new superhero saved the day.

Kung Pow Chicken was also there. He might have helped. A little.

KUNG POW CHICKEN★

Look at the picture on page 173. Why is Gordon's walk to school stranger than normal?

Why is Birdbrain turning chickens into zombies?

How does Beak Girl help Kung Pow Chicken and Egg Drop? How do Kung Pow Chicken and Egg Drop feel about her?

What is the difference between the words <u>smart</u> and <u>smartest</u>? What does the suffix <u>-est</u> mean?

Pretend you are a sidekick like Egg Drop. Design your costume and describe your superpower.

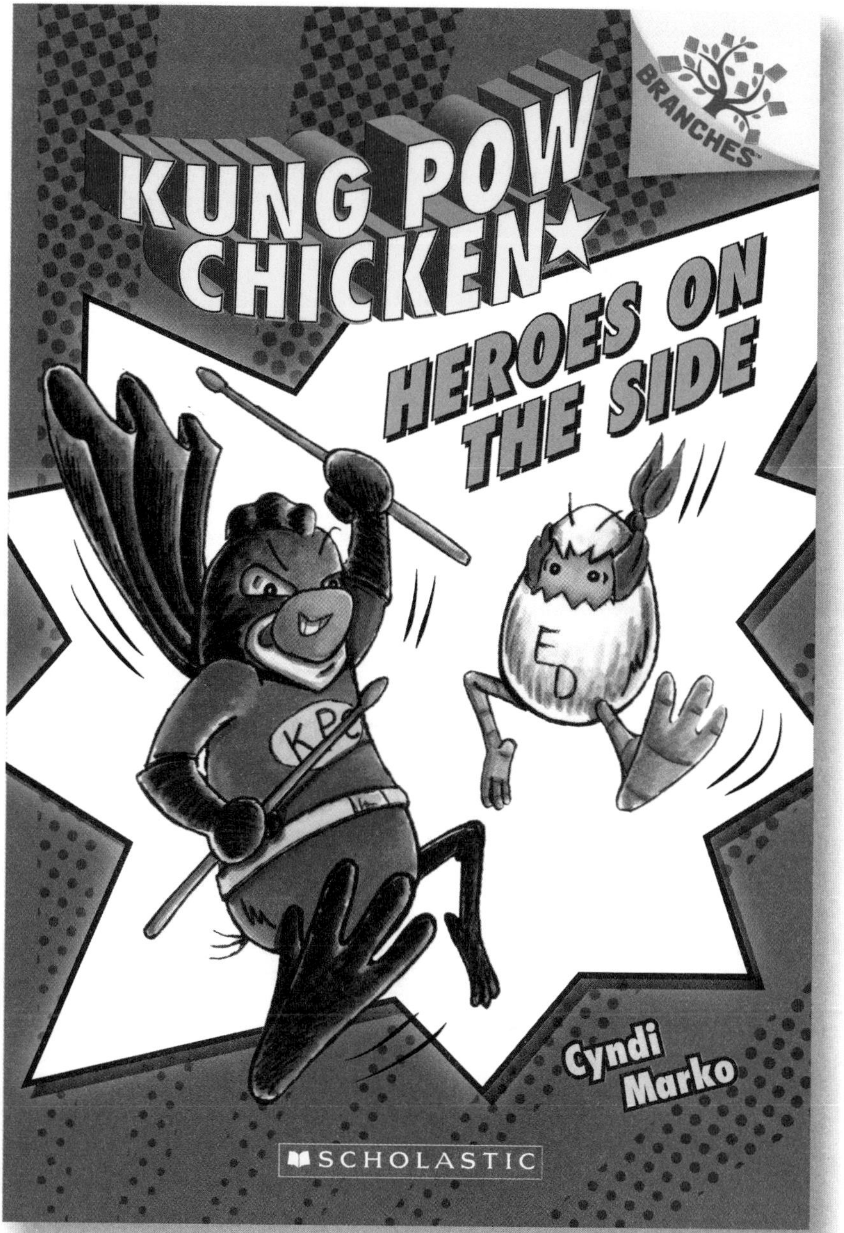
BRANCHES
KUNG POW CHICKEN
HEROES ON THE SIDE
ED
KPC
Cyndi Marko
SCHOLASTIC

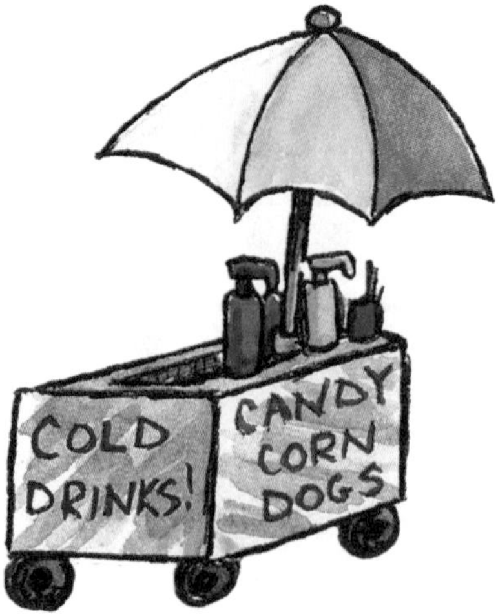
COLD
DRINKS!
CANDY
CORN
DOGS

TABLE OF CONTENTS

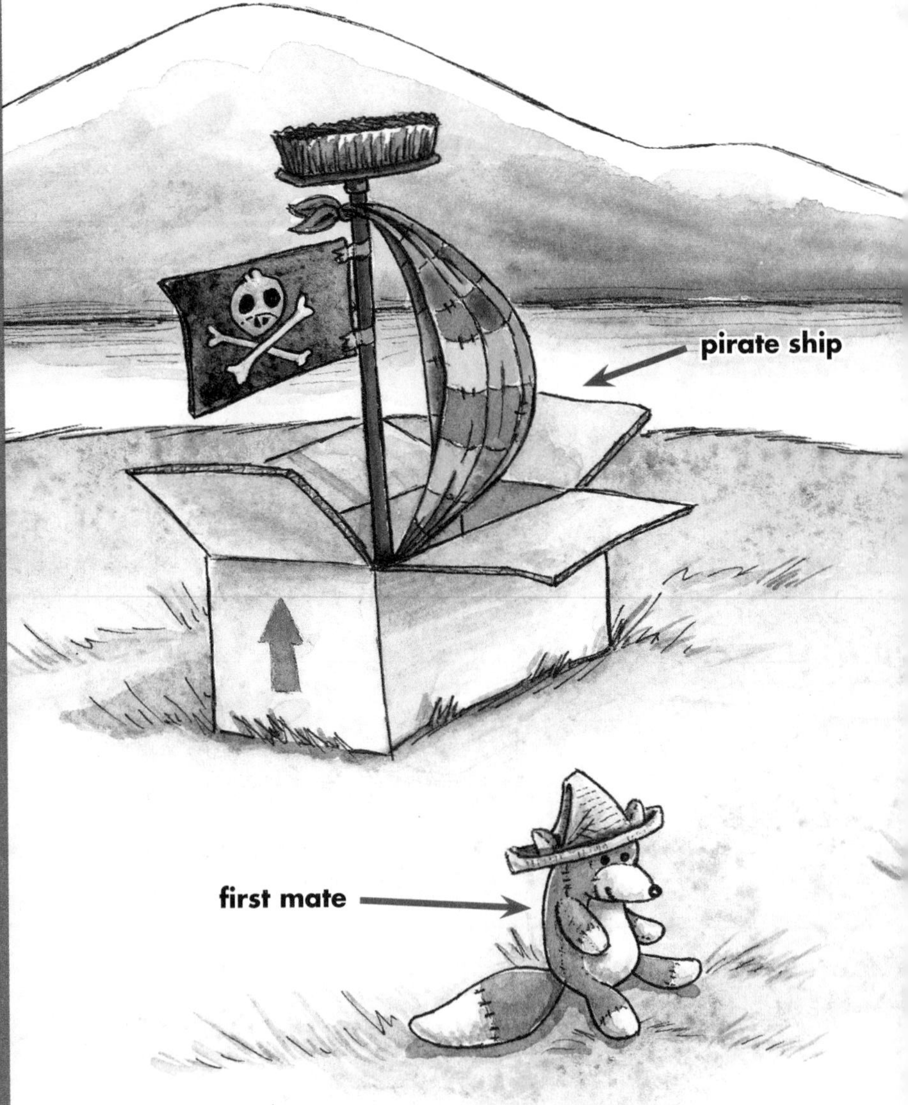
pirate ship
first mate

The Big Egg

city of Fowladelphia

pirate sword

comb

wattle

pirate sash

tail feathers

buried treasure (lunch box)

Gordon Blue seemed like an ordinary chicken.

Gordon had an ordinary family. (Most of the time.)

And he liked ordinary things.

My favorite comic.

I ♥ my bike.

I caught a fish!

But Gordon had a <u>super</u> secret.

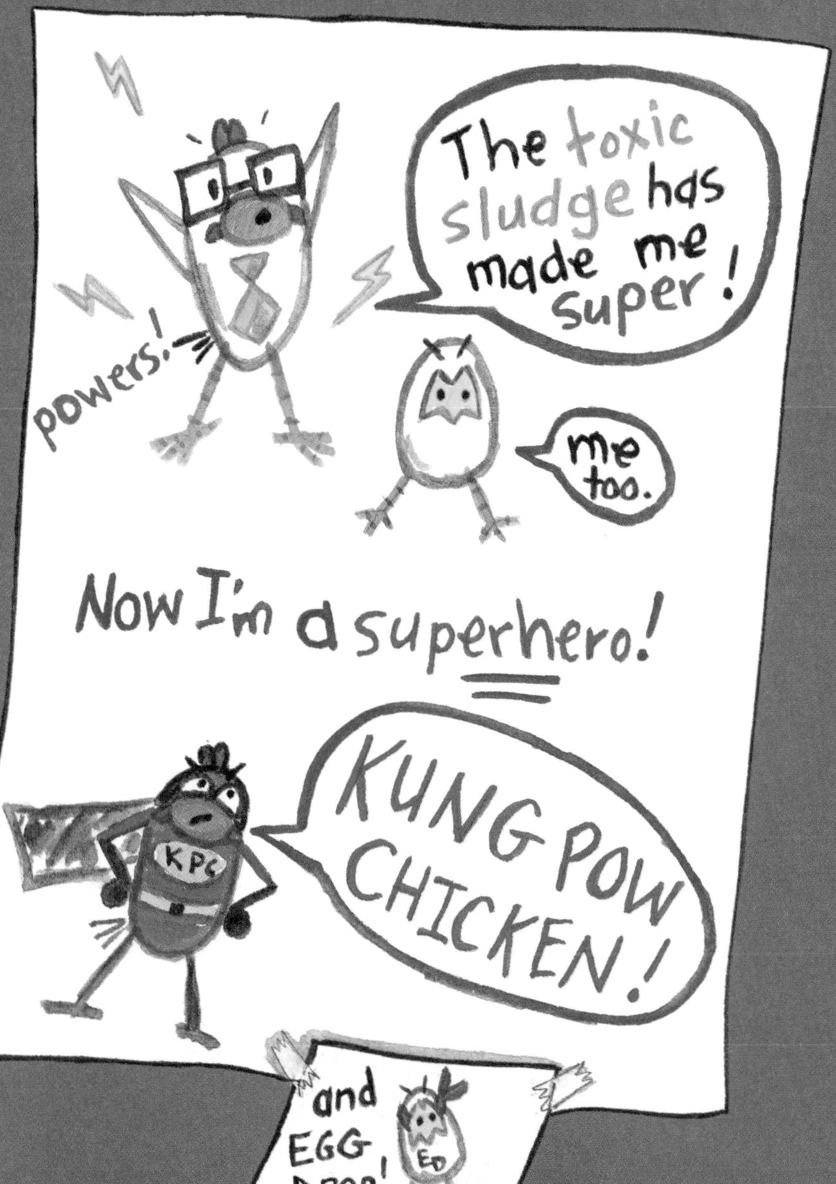
The toxic sludge has made me super powers!
me too.
Now I'm a superhero!
KPC
KUNG POW CHICKEN!
and EGG DROP!
ED

Uncle Quack was the <u>only</u> chicken who knew Gordon's <u>super</u> secret. And everyone knew that Uncle Quack helped Kung Pow Chicken catch bad guys.

Gordon liked having superpowers. But it was <u>super</u> hard being a superhero.

Gordon's mom called when he was battling bad guys.

You're late!

Some people thought anyone could be a superhero.

And he had to put up with a cheeky sidekick.

Gordon loved chasing bad guys in his city. But today, the Blue family was getting ready to go on a trip to New Yolk City.

New Yolk has the <u>best</u> superhero! I hope I'll get to meet Rubber Rooster. He's super cool!

So is his sidekick, Radar!

How does Rubber Rooster keep his leotard from sticking?

Thank you for reading SUPERHERO MONTHLY

Radar & Rubber Rooster

Gordon and Benny went to the lab to help their uncle pack.

Um, I don't think there's room for that.

I can't wait to go skating in New Yolk!

Oh! I almost forgot! A flyer came in the mail for Egg Drop.

Benny took the flyer from Uncle Quack.

SIDEKICK
SUPER★CON!

Dear Egg Drop,

You are invited to a party! Radar, sidekick to NYC's Rubber Rooster, is proud to host the FIRST-EVER SIDEKICK SUPER-CON! Eat yummy lunch and dessert! Dance and play games with other sidekicks! And see who will win the SIDEKICK OF THE YEAR award!

 WHEN: Saturday at 1 PM

WHERE: Birdy Ballroom

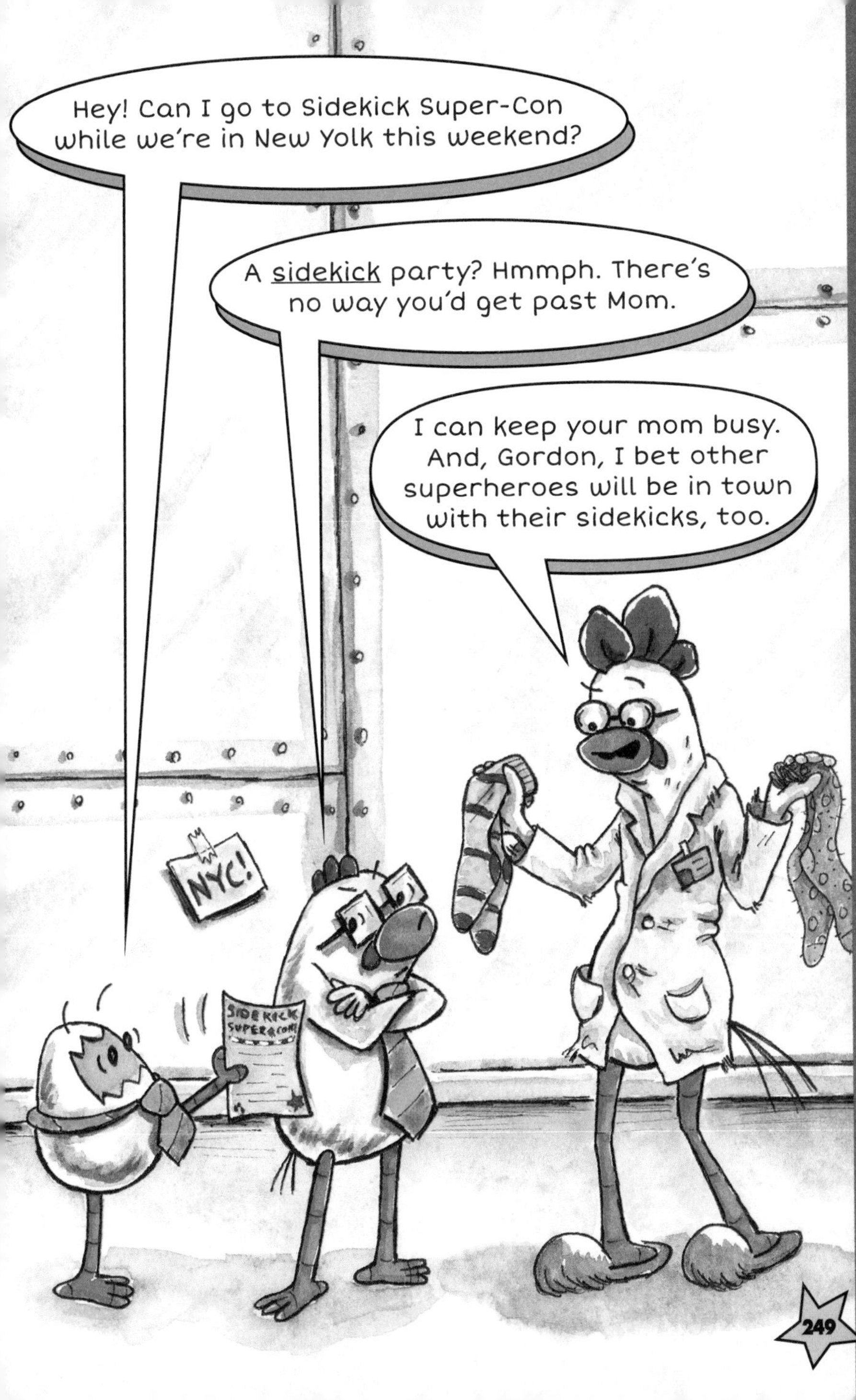
Hey! Can I go to Sidekick Super-Con while we're in New Yolk this weekend?
A sidekick party? Hmmph. There's no way you'd get past Mom.
I can keep your mom busy. And, Gordon, I bet other superheroes will be in town with their sidekicks, too.
NYC!
SIDEKICK SUPER CON!

Gordon and Benny went home to do their own packing.

The boys were too excited to sleep.

Fowl Air

2

On Friday morning, the Blue family boarded a plane to New Yolk City!

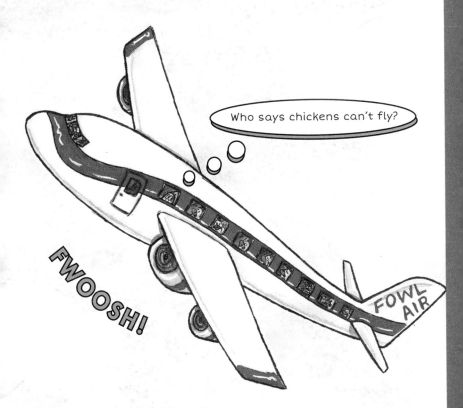

They took a cab from the airport.

They all dropped off their luggage at the Roostervelt Hotel.

Then Mrs. Blue dashed off to the fancy shops. And Uncle Quack took his nephews ice-skating.

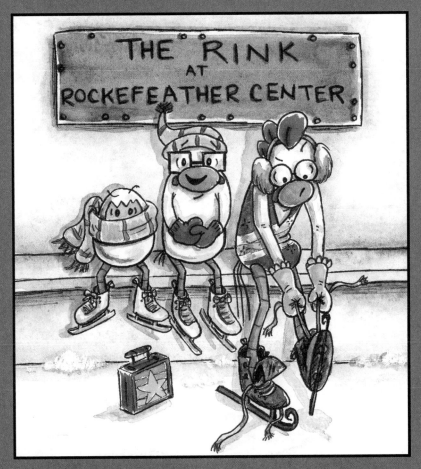

They were all having fun on the ice.

I can really rock a leotard!

Suddenly, Gordon's tail feathers started to tingle. He knew what that meant: A bad guy was up to no good!

TINGLE!

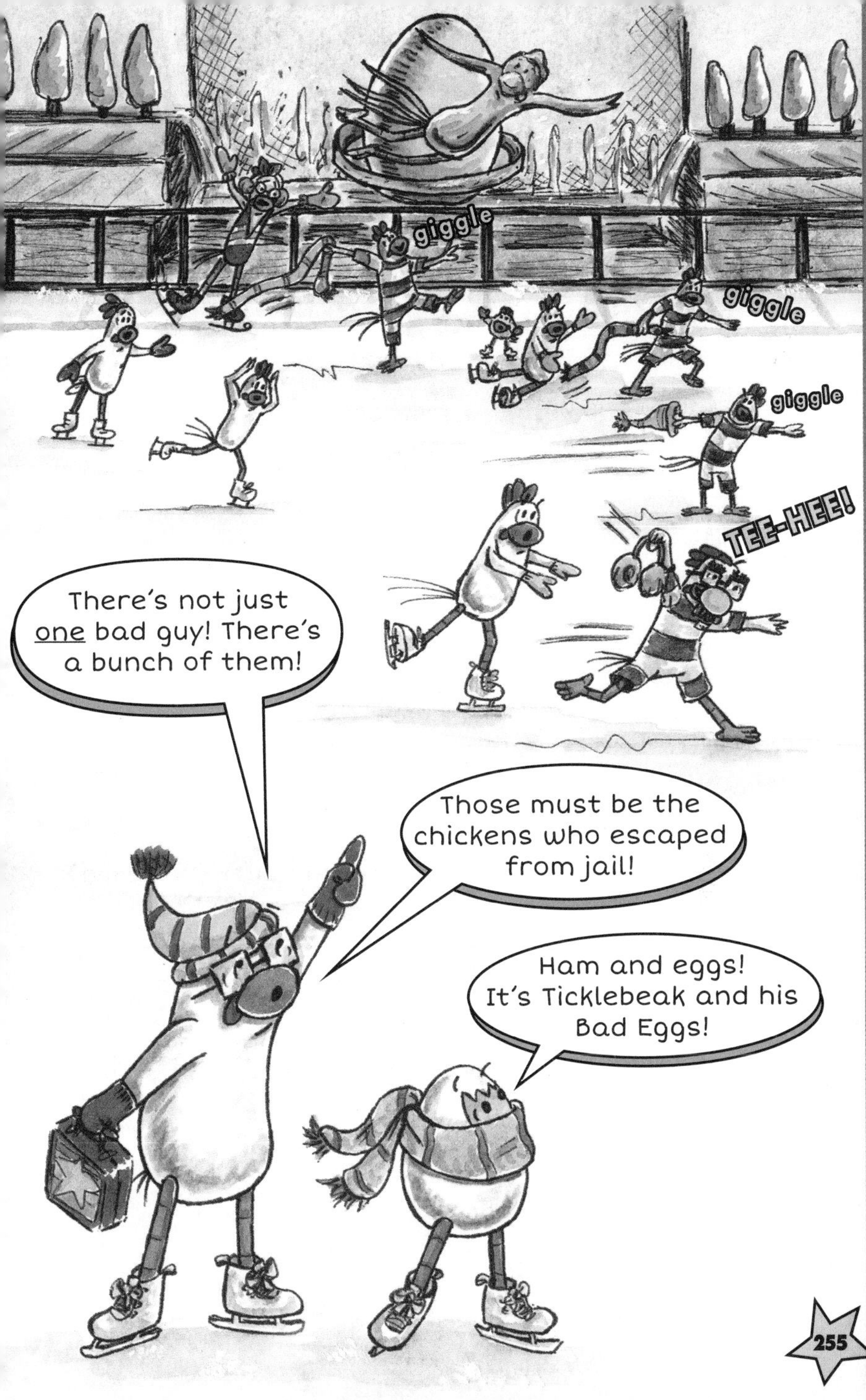
giggle
giggle
giggle
TEE-HEE!
There's not just one bad guy! There's a bunch of them!
Those must be the chickens who escaped from jail!
Ham and eggs! It's Ticklebeak and his Bad Eggs!

The brothers found a good place to hide. Gordon flung open his lunch box and grabbed his super suit. Benny put on his mask.

Just then, <u>another</u> superhero team burst onto the ice.

Gordon squeezed into his leotard. But he was too late. Rubber Rooster and Radar had chased the bad guys away.

Rubber Rooster was swarmed by star-struck chickens. Kung Pow Chicken wanted to meet him. But he couldn't get through the crowd.

No one's ever asked <u>you</u> to sign anything.

New Yolk is Rubber Rooster's city. Let him catch the bad guys.

Gordon and Benny stayed in the hotel room for the rest of the day. Gordon moped. Benny daydreamed.

I'd like to thank Professor Quack. And my good friend Beak Girl.

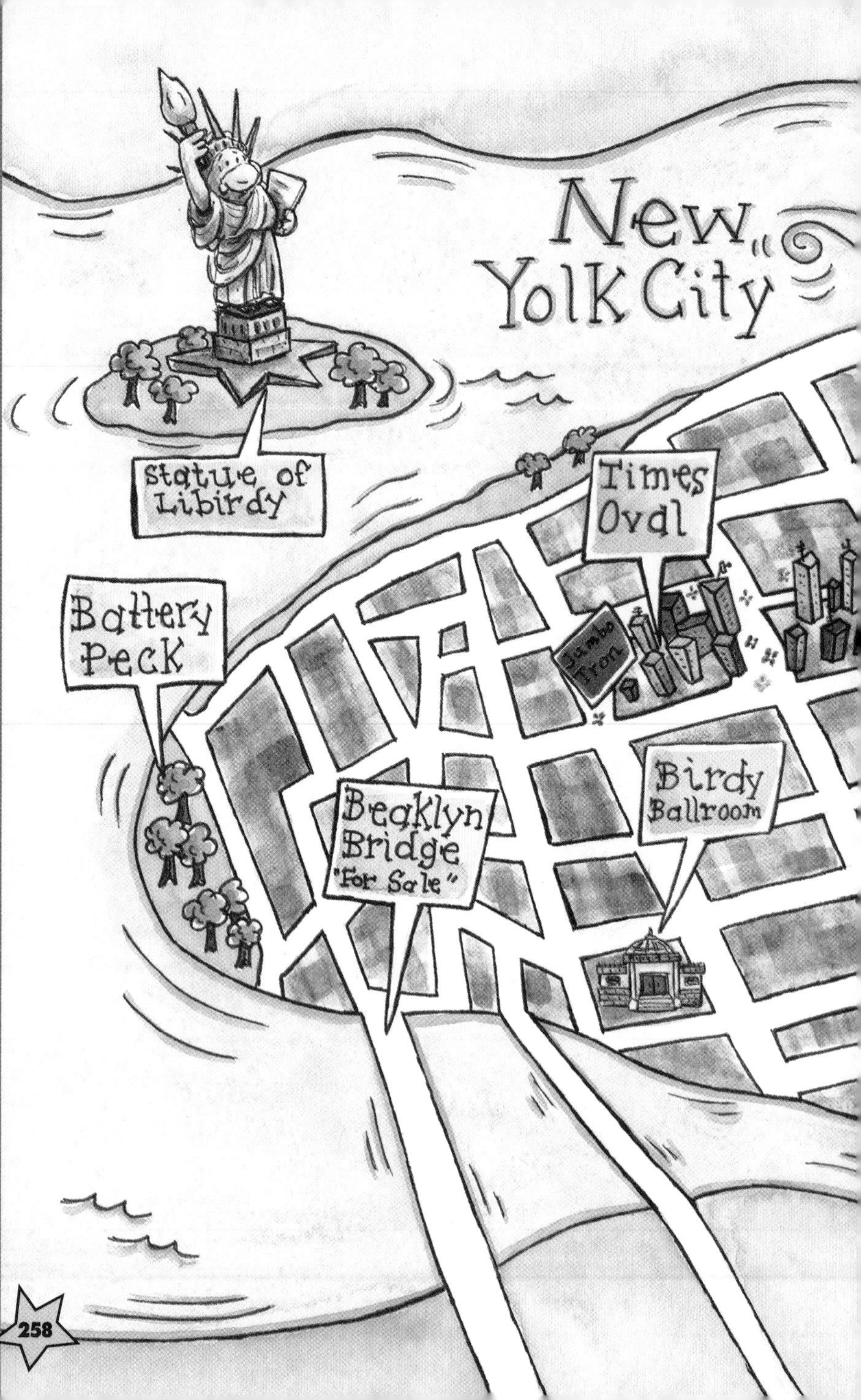
New Yolk City
Statue of Libirdy
Battery Peck
Times Oval
Jumbo Tron
Beaklyn Bridge "For Sale"
Birdy Ballroom

It's a Trap! 3

Early Saturday morning, Gordon and his family
went sight-seeing all over New Yolk City.

Then it was almost time for Sidekick Super-Con! Uncle Quack had a plan to keep Mrs. Blue busy. He was taking her to the spa for an afternoon of pampering.

Benny was ready to go in a jiffy. But Gordon wanted to look <u>extra</u> super in case he ran into other superheroes.

By the time Gordon was ready, Benny was in a tizzy.

They rushed
out of the room
and down the
hall.

Gordon
hummed along
with the elevator
music.

Then they
scrambled
through the
lobby.

And the
doorman
hailed them
a cab.

BOK!

HOTEL

The cab headed to Sidekick Super-Con.
Gordon was excited to visit the Statue of Libirdy
after he dropped off Benny.

The cab zoomed in and out of traffic. Gordon and Benny bokked about the trapped sidekicks.

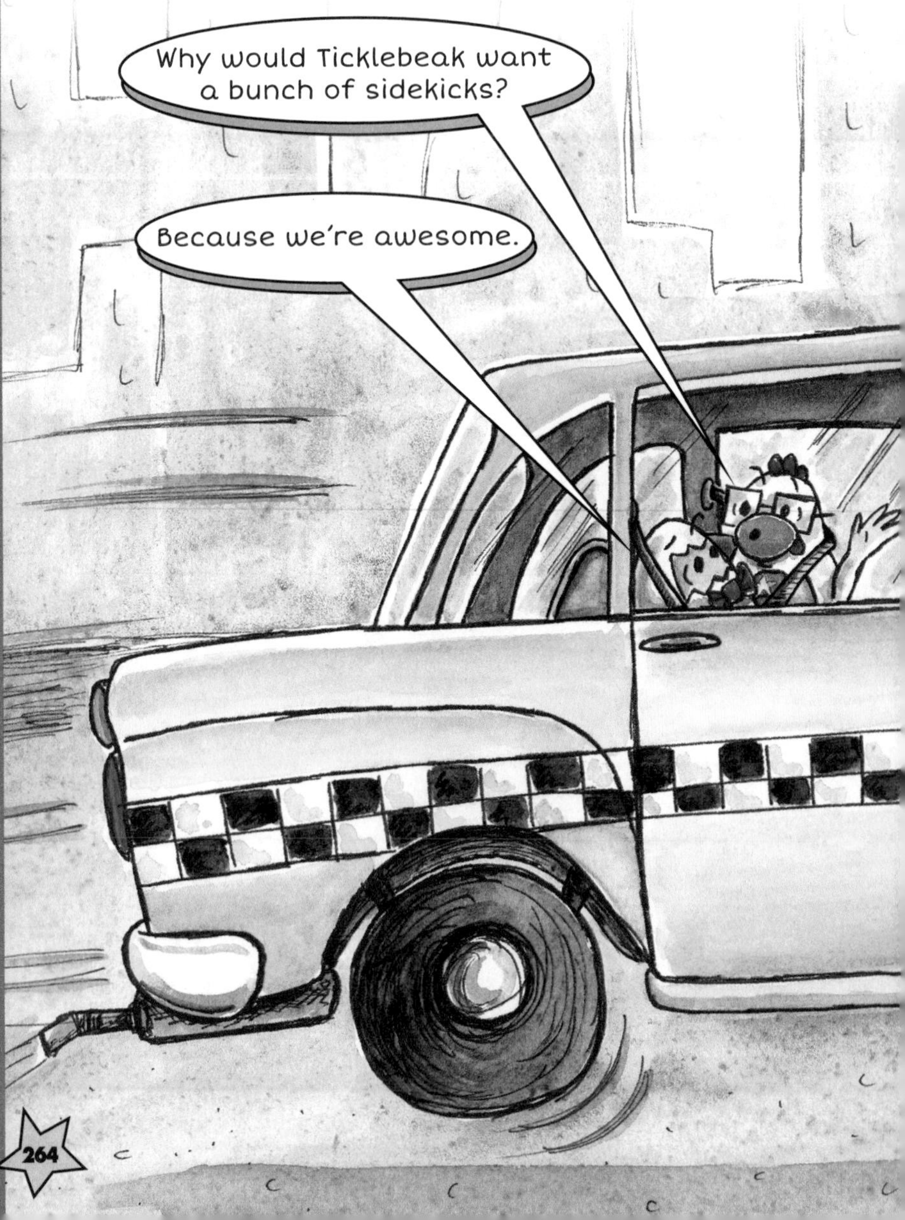
Why would Ticklebeak want a bunch of sidekicks?
Because we're awesome.

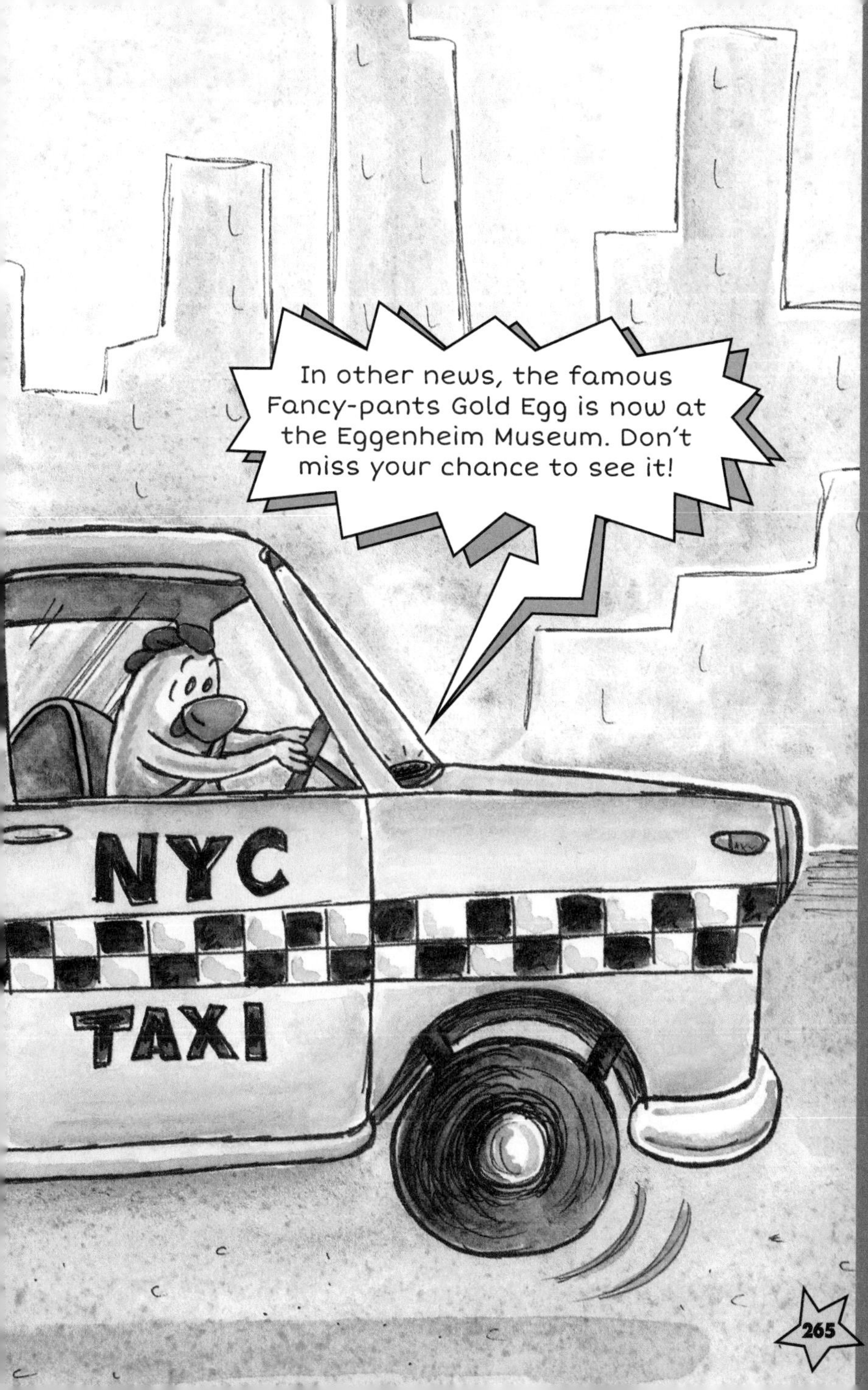
In other news, the famous Fancy-pants Gold Egg is now at the Eggenheim Museum. Don't miss your chance to see it!
NYC
TAXI

The cab skidded to a stop near the Birdy Ballroom. Gordon paid the taxi driver.

They put on their super suits.

Kung Pow Chicken jumped out, ready to battle! Egg Drop was already off and running.

Two Bad Eggs stood guard. The heroes tiptoed around the building to look for another way in.

Kung Pow Chicken slipped around the corner.
He crashed into another hero.

But Rubber Rooster and Kung Pow Chicken did not seem to notice Egg Drop. They had important <u>super</u> stuff to talk about.

Wow. I really like your leotard.

Thanks. I made it myself.

Do you have a problem with wedgies?

Oh, for peep's sake.

Soon more superheroes showed up. They all had sidekicks trapped in the Birdy Ballroom.

While the superheroes were busy bokking, Ticklebeak and some Bad Eggs tried to sneak away. One of the Bad Eggs giggled.

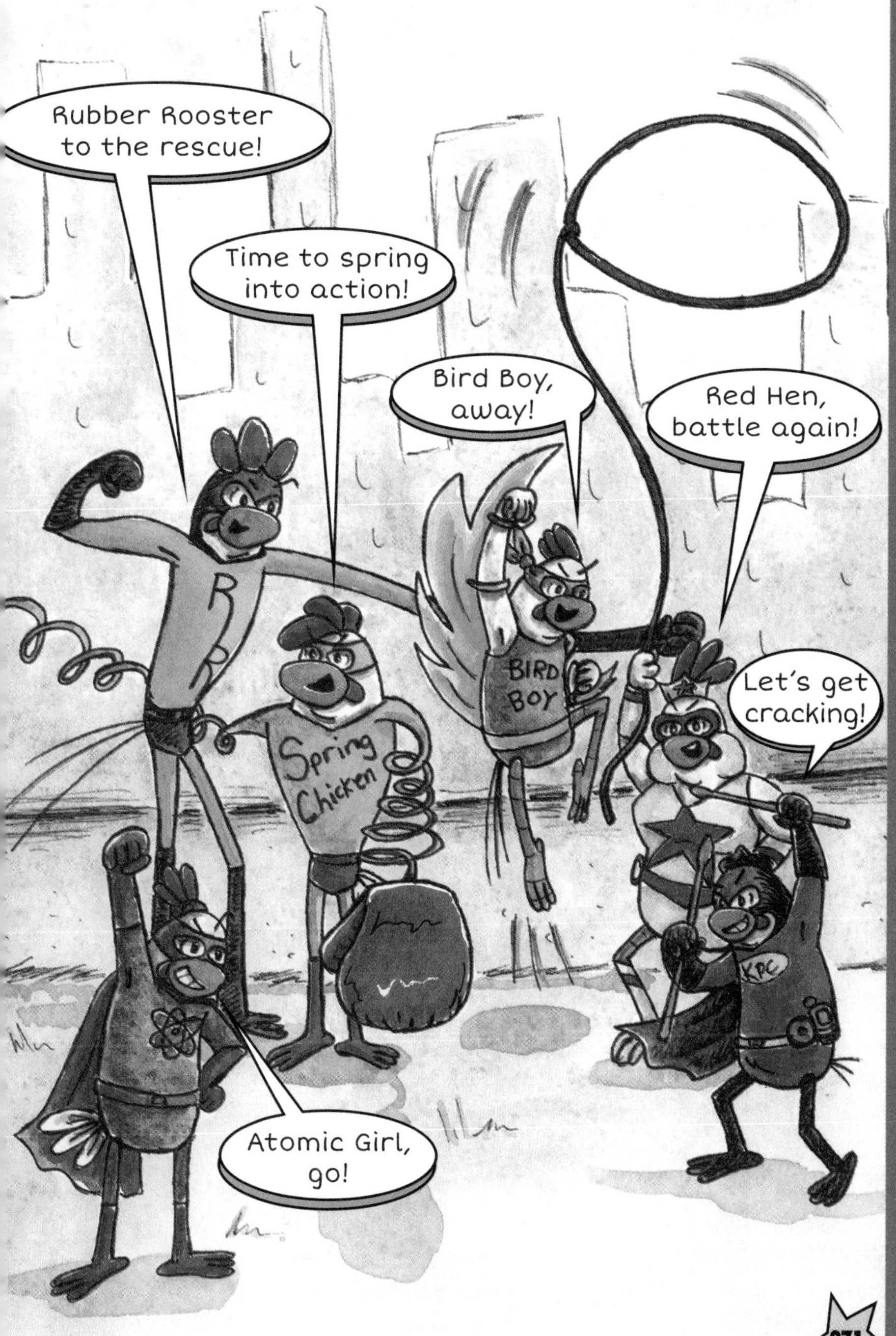
Rubber Rooster to the rescue!
Time to spring into action!
Bird Boy, away!
Red Hen, battle again!
Let's get cracking!
Atomic Girl, go!
Spring Chicken
BIRD BOY
KPC

The good guys got in a super-mega battle with the bad guys!

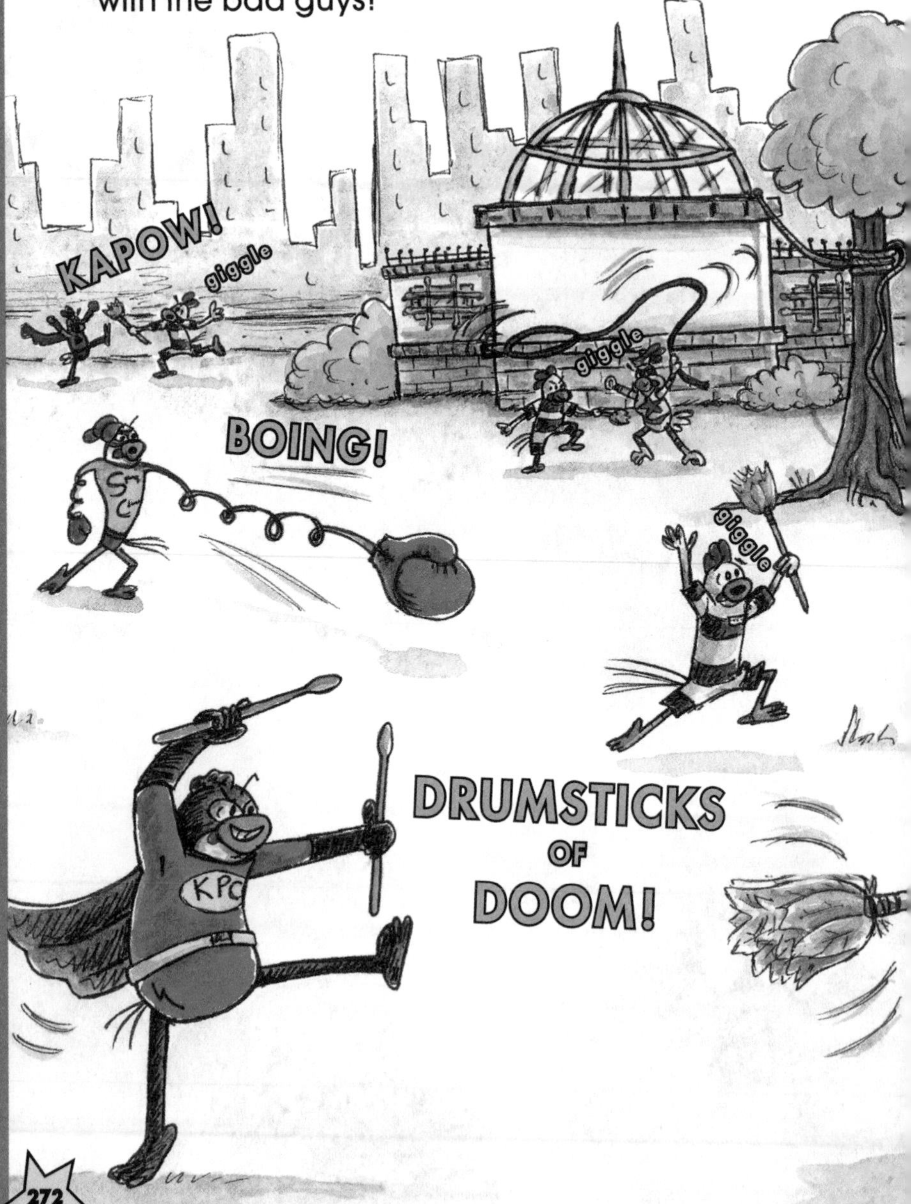
KAPOW!
giggle
giggle
BOING!
giggle
DRUMSTICKS
OF
DOOM!

The battle raged on and on.

But the bad guys got away.

The other superheroes went off after the
bad guys. But Kung Pow Chicken and Egg Drop
were hungry.

The heroes ate pie and tried to figure out what to do next.

This pie is really good.

You've got berries on your beak.

RIIIING!!

Kung Pow Chicken answered his Beak-Phone.

275

It was Uncle Quack.

I have news! Ticklebeak's Bad Eggs are playing pranks all over the city! The other superheroes haven't been able to catch them! And the heroes' sidekicks are still trapped!

There's no way into that building! We'll need a gadget, Uncle Quack! Can you make something to help us get inside to rescue the sidekicks?

I'll get to work. Your mom is soaking in a mud bath. Oh! And the radio said no one has seen Ticklebeak.

Kung Pow Chicken put away his phone.

The heroes rushed to the subway.

The Bad Eggs had been busy. They had hit all the hot spots in the city: the Statue of Libirdy, the New Yolk Public Library, and even Rockefeather Center.

First, Kung Pow Chicken and Egg Drop went to the Statue of Libirdy.

The Statue of Libirdy doesn't wear bloomers!

It's pretty funny though.

tee hee hee

The Bad Eggs had made a mess of the statue. But they hadn't left any clues to where Ticklebeak could be.

279

Next, the heroes went to the public library.

Then Kung Pow Chicken and Egg Drop went back to Rockefeather Center. Now the ice rink was filled with gooey white stuff.

The superheroes searched high and low. Finally, they spotted a clue.

It's a flyer for the Eggenheim Museum. Ticklebeak and his gang must be there!

Let's go!

As soon as the heroes reached the museum, Kung Pow Chicken's tail feathers started to tingle. Then Kung Pow Chicken and Egg Drop heard goofy giggling. They hid.

Ticklebeak and some Bad Eggs! What were they doing in the museum?

EGGENHEIM MUSEUM

giggle

giggle

giggle

Look! Ticklebeak has the Fancy-pants Gold Egg!

TINGLE!

283

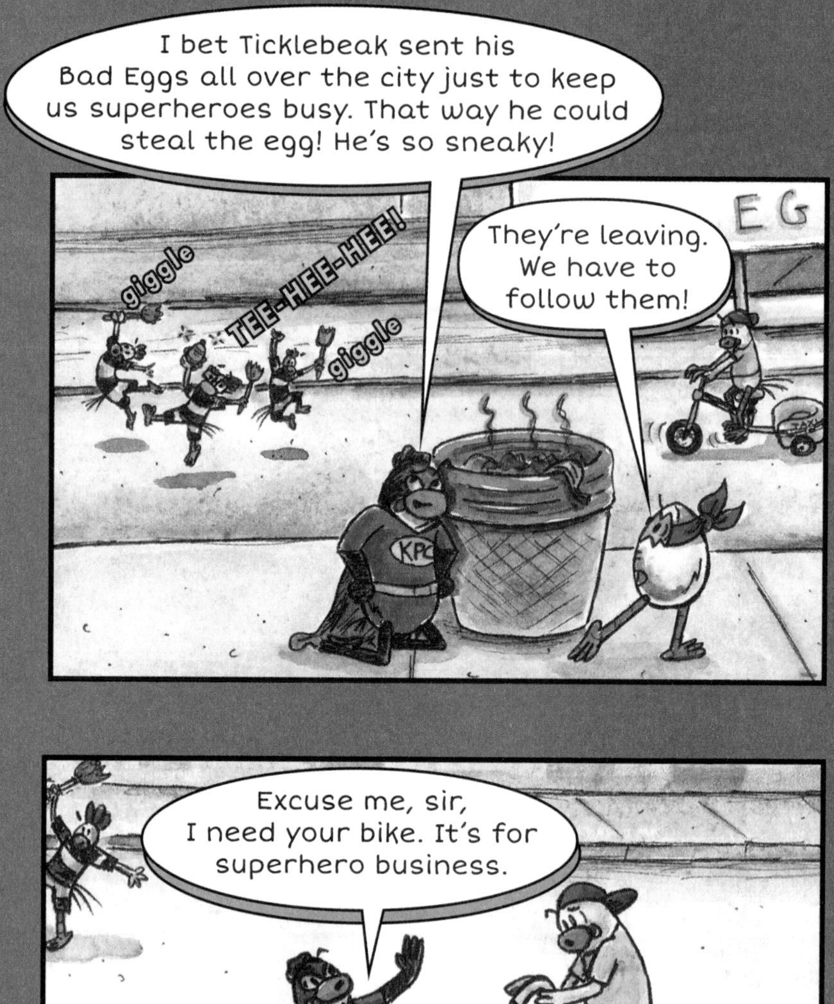
I bet Ticklebeak sent his Bad Eggs all over the city just to keep us superheroes busy. That way he could steal the egg! He's so sneaky!
giggle
TEE-HEE-HEE!
giggle
E G
They're leaving. We have to follow them!
KPC
Excuse me, sir, I need your bike. It's for superhero business.
TAXI

Super-silly string

Kung Pow Chicken and Egg Drop followed
Ticklebeak and the Bad Eggs all the way to
Times Oval.

Times Oval was full of Bad Eggs. They were making a mess.

Just then, the other superheroes showed up.
Kung Pow Chicken waved them over.

What do we do?

We fight!

Yes!

Egg Drop, stay here. You'll just be in our way.

Hmph. That was _super_ mean.

The superheroes jumped out from behind the potted shrub. Egg Drop stayed hidden as Kung Pow Chicken and his super friends charged into battle.

Egg Drop watched the superheroes fight with all their might.

Then he watched them all get caught! Without their sidekicks, the heroes were easily trapped.

A Bad Egg sprayed Kung Pow Chicken's beak shut with Super-Silly String.

Egg Drop had to free the superheroes. But he needed help. He needed sidekicks.

Egg Drop slipped away. He rushed back to the hotel. Uncle Quack would know what to do.

Ticklebeak and his Bad Eggs have chick-napped Gordon—and the other superheroes, too! I'm the <u>only</u> one who can save them!

And, um, I don't think those cucumbers are for eating.

HOTEL SPA "FOR PUFFY EYES"

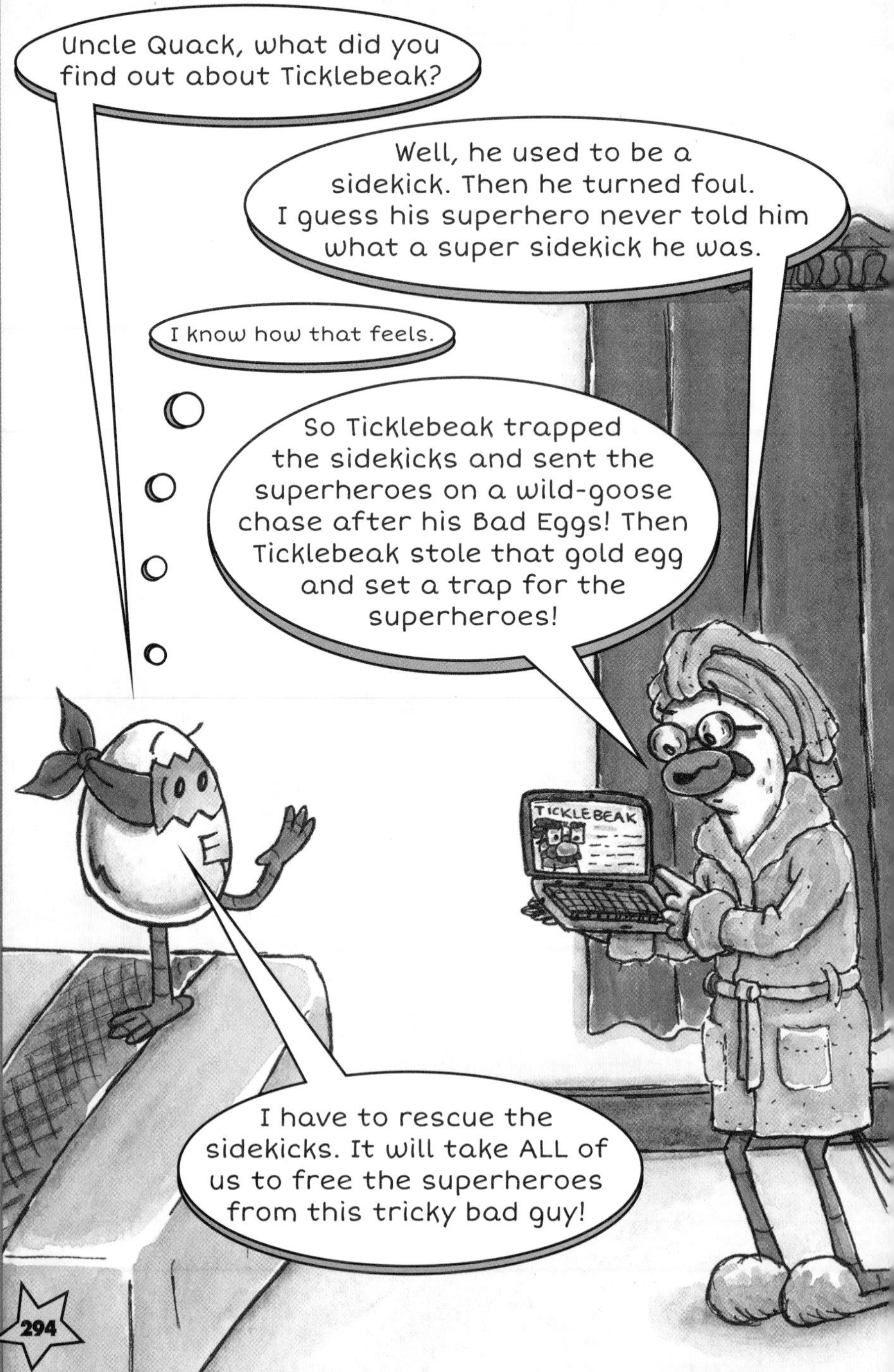
Uncle Quack, what did you find out about Ticklebeak?
Well, he used to be a sidekick. Then he turned foul. I guess his superhero never told him what a super sidekick he was.
I know how that feels.
So Ticklebeak trapped the sidekicks and sent the superheroes on a wild-goose chase after his Bad Eggs! Then Ticklebeak stole that gold egg and set a trap for the superheroes!
TICKLEBEAK
I have to rescue the sidekicks. It will take ALL of us to free the superheroes from this tricky bad guy!

Uncle Quack had been busy working on a new gadget.

This gadget should help you rescue the sidekicks. It's a super disguise called the Pi-ZZZ-a Guy™. I baked a yummy cheesy pizza. And I warmed a jug of milk. Together, these should make those Bad Eggs super sleepy!

I'll keep your mom busy at the spa. Good luck.

Thanks!

Egg Drop pedaled the bicycle taxi to the Birdy Ballroom. Then he took a big breath and climbed up the front steps.

The Bad Eggs shrugged. They gobbled up the pizza. They gulped down the warm milk. Then their tummies were full and they fell asleep.

Egg Drop grabbed the key and unlocked the door.

The sidekicks were very happy to see Egg Drop.

Egg Drop had a plan. He told it to the sidekicks.
Then they took the subway to Times Oval.

The sidekicks burst up out of the subway.

They jumped right into battle with Ticklebeak's Bad Eggs.

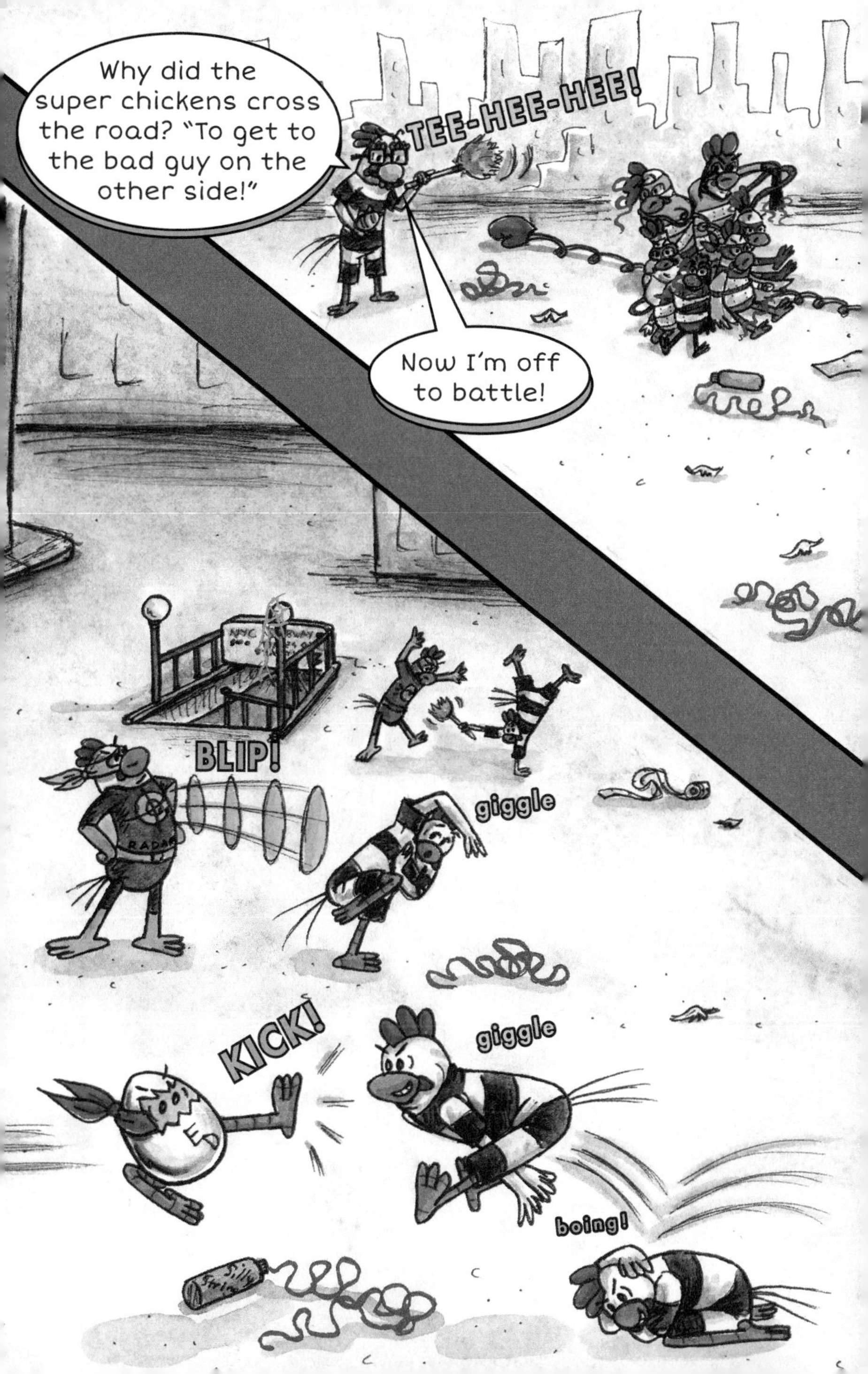
Why did the super chickens cross the road? "To get to the bad guy on the other side!"
TEE-HEE-HEE!
Now I'm off to battle!
BLIP!
giggle
KICK!
giggle
boing!

Egg Drop and Radar slipped away from the
fight. They ran over to free the superheroes.
Egg Drop scraped the Super-Silly String from
Kung Pow Chicken's beak.

Kung Pow, use
your Power Peck!

PECK! PECK!

The superheroes were free of
Ticklebeak's messy trap in no time.

Good work, Radar!

You, too, Egg Drop.
But what took you
so long? Now, let's
get cracking!

The big battle continued. Then Ticklebeak stepped forward. He bokked loudly. Everyone stopped fighting so they could hear better.

But jail was no fun. Ticklebeak would not go back without a fight! Kung Pow Chicken flashed his Drumsticks of Doom.

The Bad Eggs rushed at the superheroes. The heroes were outnumbered.

But the sidekicks were ready! They tossed rolls of Ultra-Mega Toilet Paper to their superheroes. And they sprayed cans of Super-Silly String.

ZZZZZIP!

OF MICE AND CHICKENS

SPISH!

SPISH!

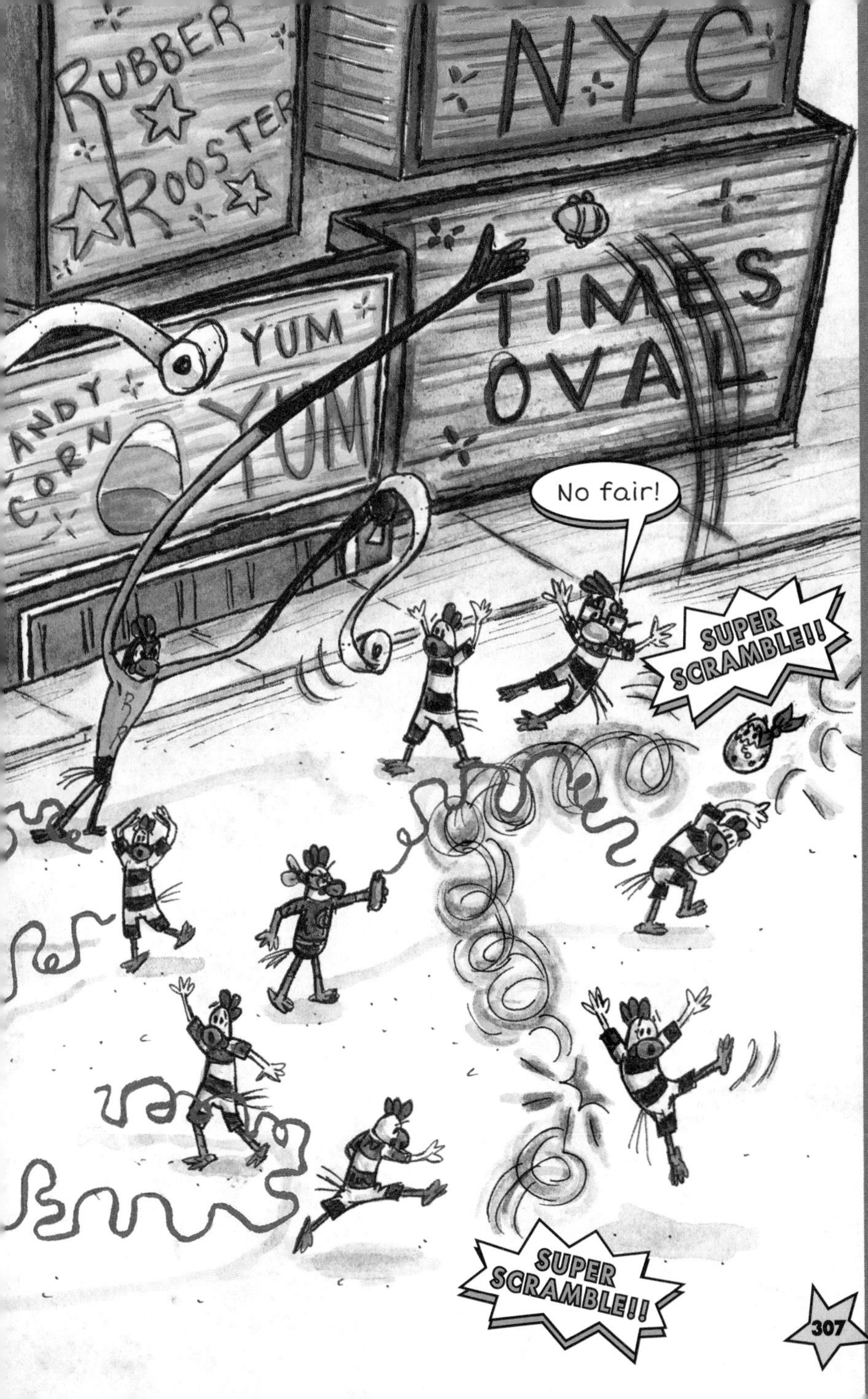
RUBBER ROOSTER
NYC
YUM
ANDY CORN
YUM
TIMES OVAL
No fair!
SUPER SCRAMBLE!!
SUPER SCRAMBLE!!

The sidekicks and superheroes put Ticklebeak and all of his Bad Eggs in one basket.

The good guys said their good-byes. Radar gave Egg Drop a high five.

Kung Pow Chicken and Egg Drop took off
their super suits and ran back to the hotel.
Mrs. Blue gave her boys a big hug.

The next morning, the Blue family flew home
to Fowladelphia. Gordon and Benny went with
Uncle Quack to the lab. A surprise was waiting
for Egg Drop.

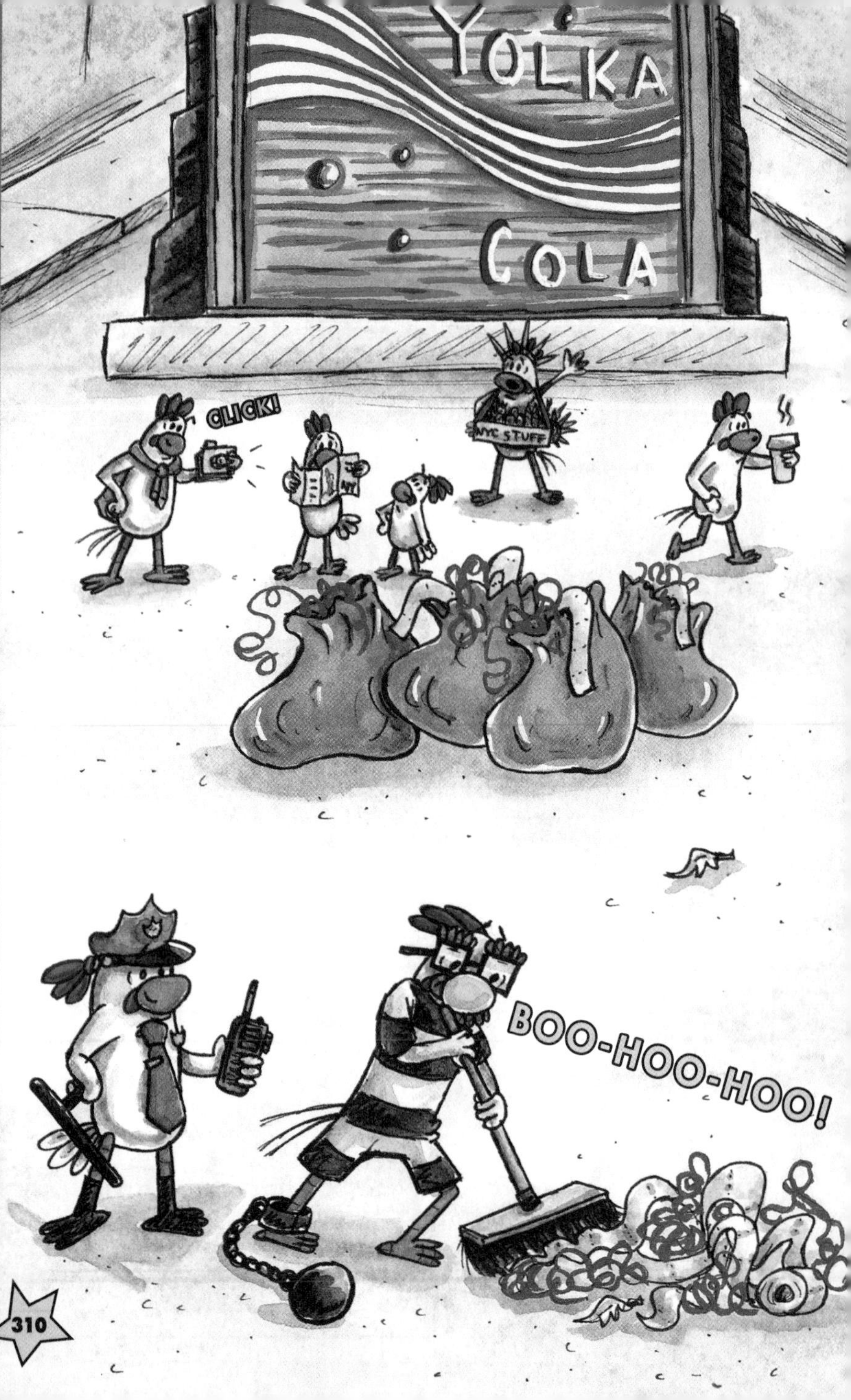
YOLKA
COLA
CLICK!
NYC STUFF
BOO-HOO-HOO!